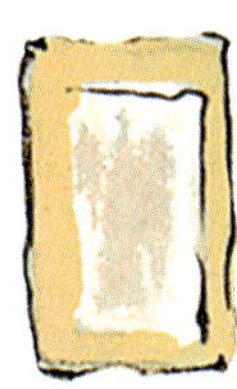

*'It's no good. He always draws us when we least expect it.*

*And sometimes the results are embarrassing!'*

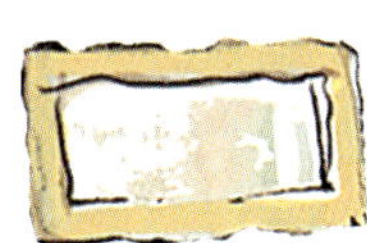

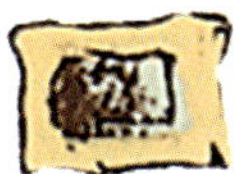

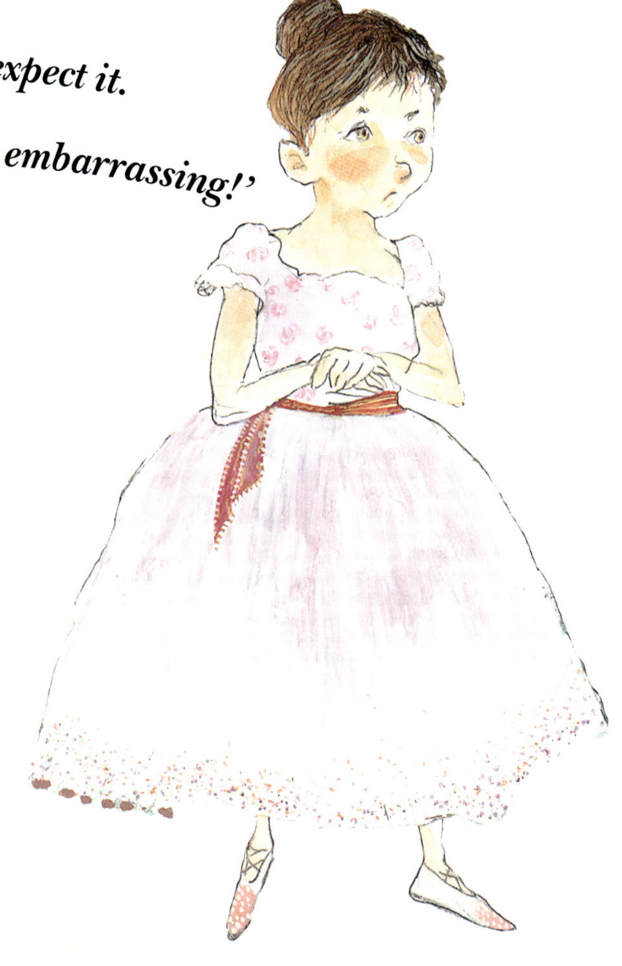

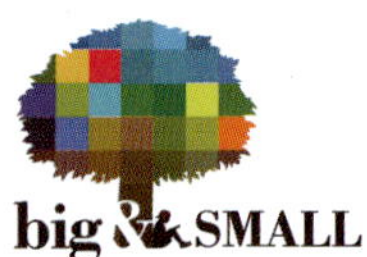


Original Korean text by Mi-ae Kim
Illustrations by Dong-il Jang


This English edition published by big & SMALL in 2017
by arrangement with Aram Publishing
English text edited by Scott Forbes


ISBN: 978-1-925234-68-8

Printed in Korea

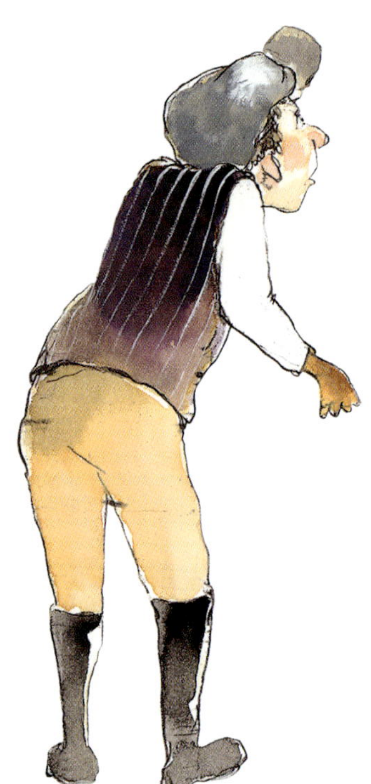

# The Quiet Observer

## THE ART OF DEGAS

Written by Mi-ae Kim
Illustrated by Dong-il Jang
Edited by Scott Forbes

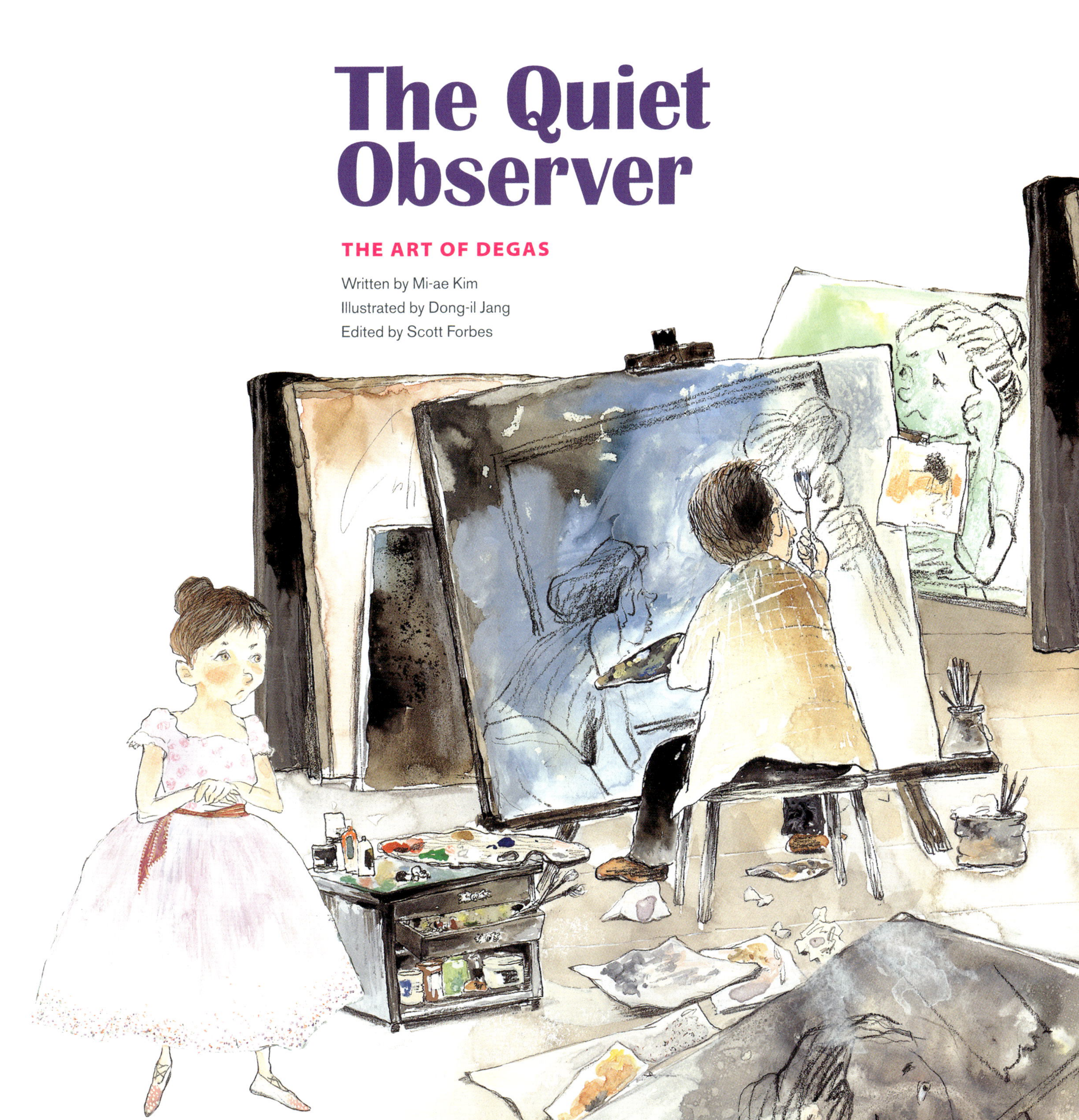

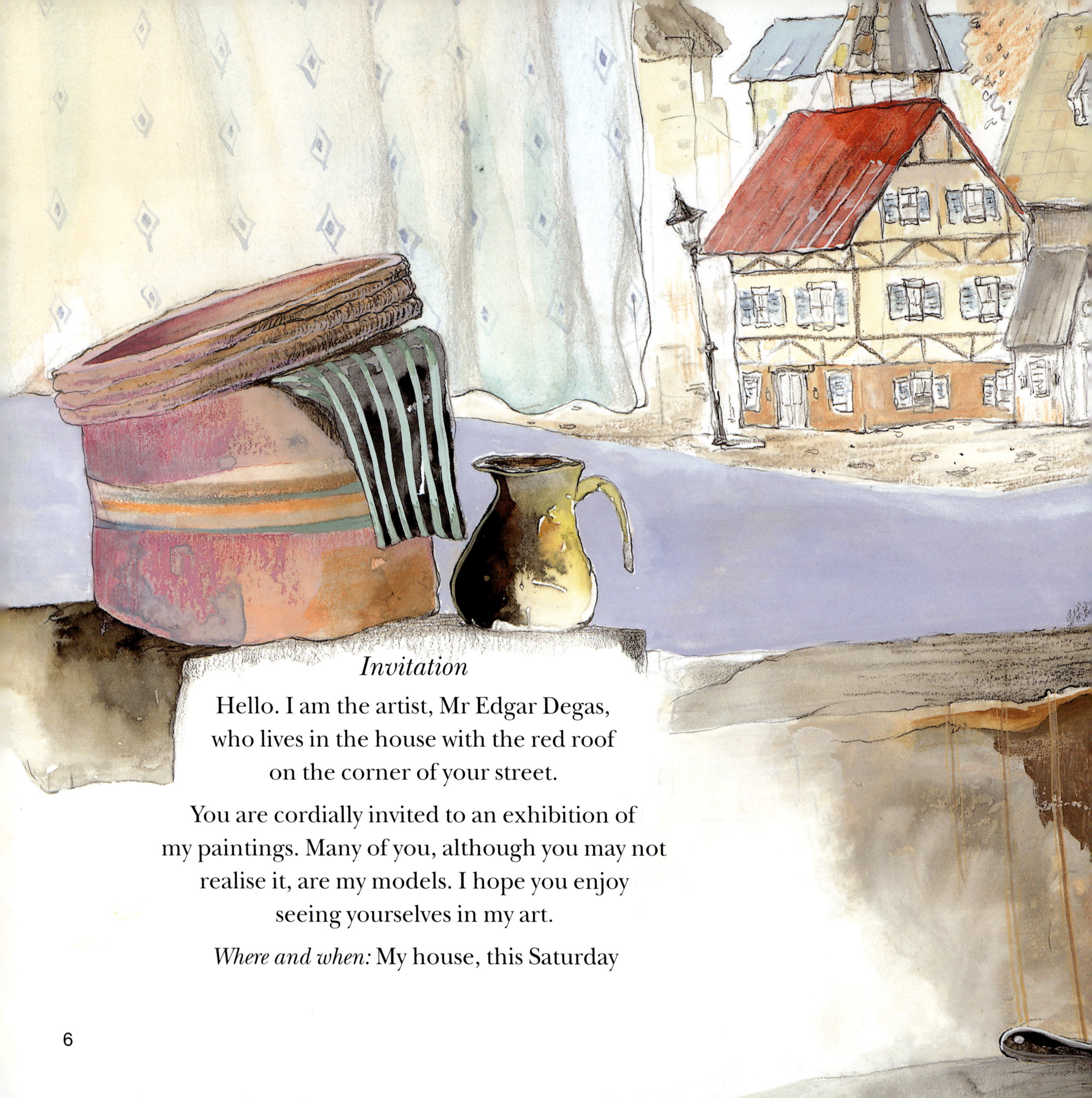

*Invitation*

Hello. I am the artist, Mr Edgar Degas, who lives in the house with the red roof on the corner of your street.

You are cordially invited to an exhibition of my paintings. Many of you, although you may not realise it, are my models. I hope you enjoy seeing yourselves in my art.

*Where and when:* My house, this Saturday

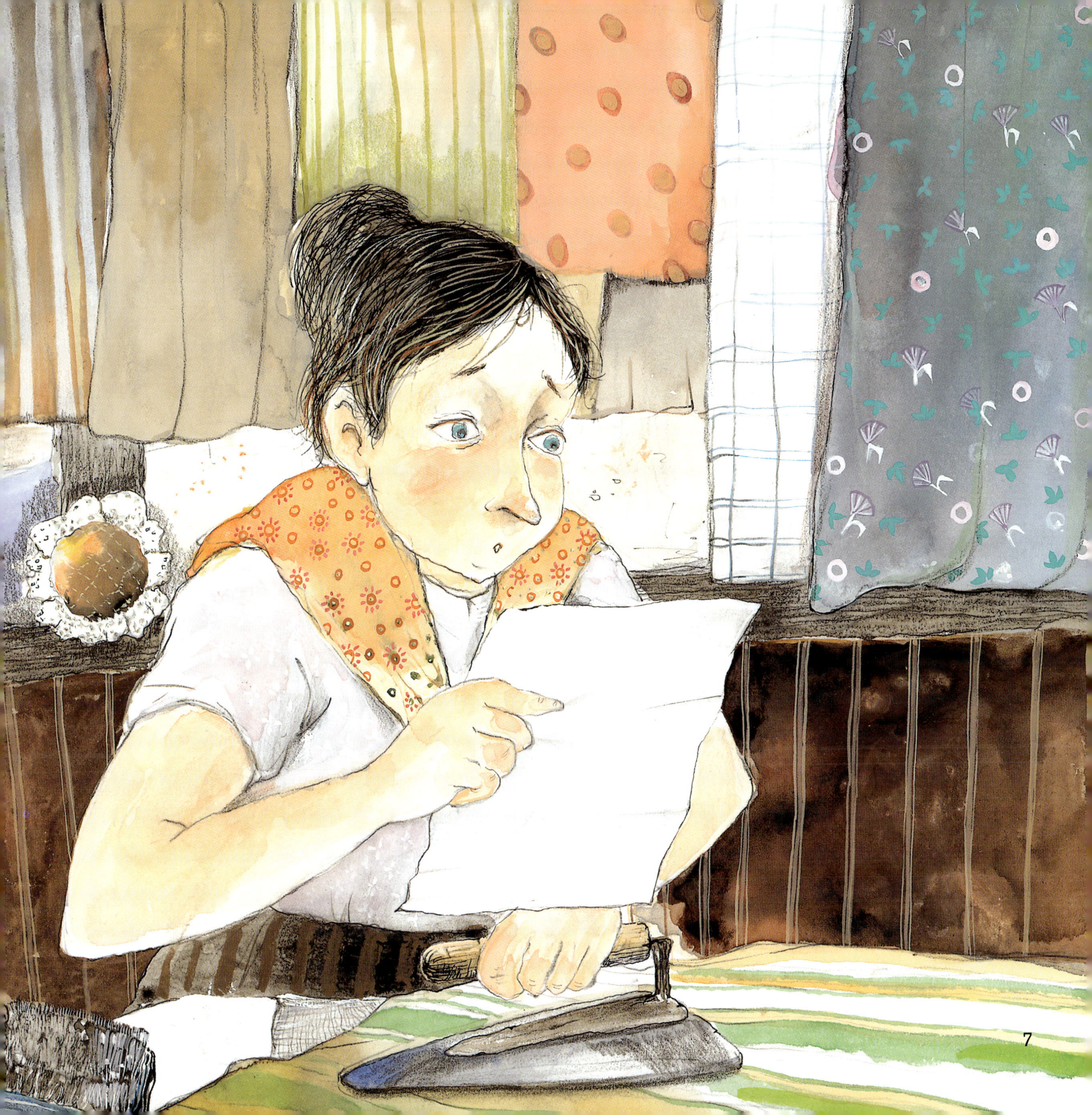

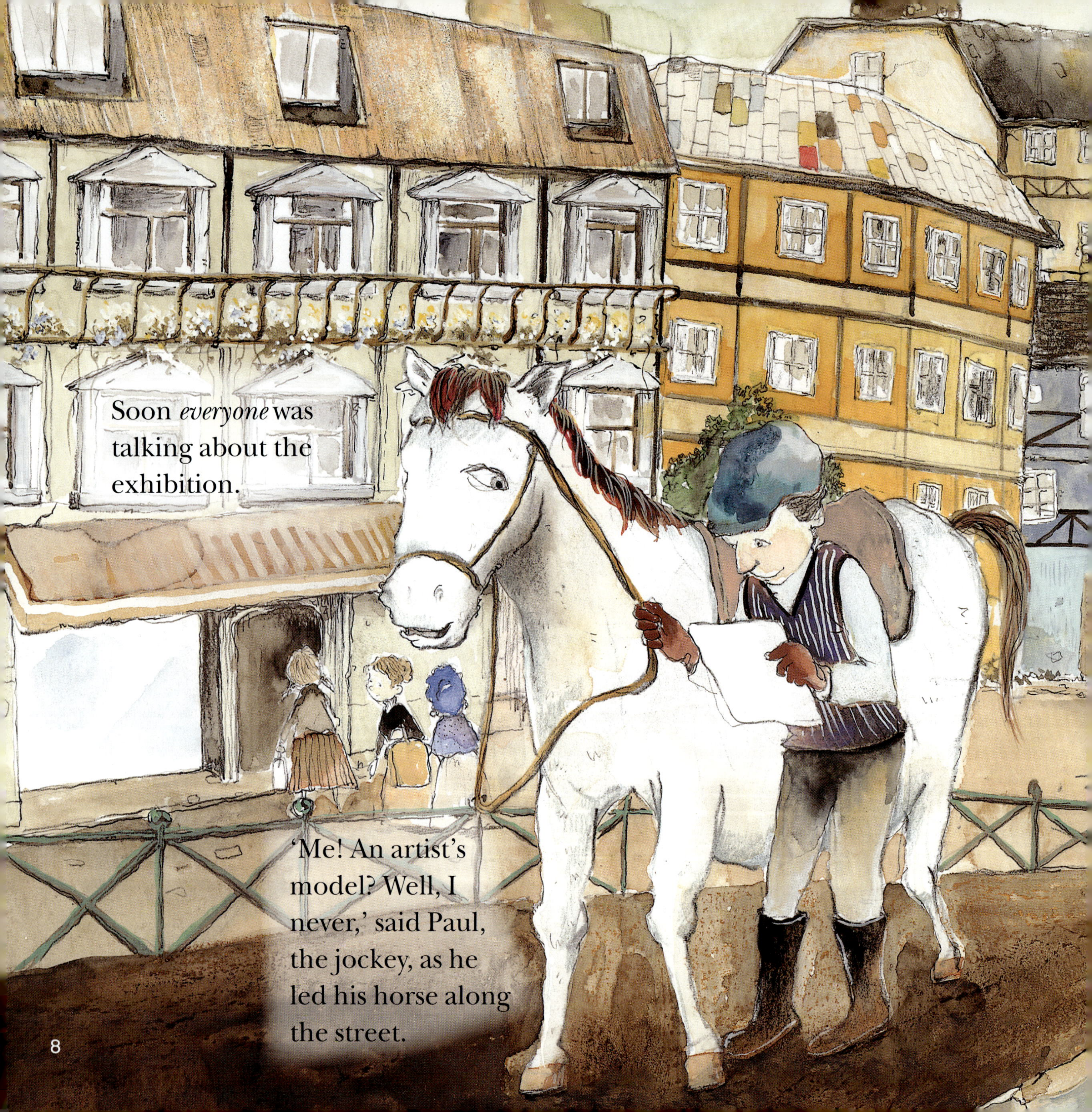

Soon *everyone* was talking about the exhibition.

'Me! An artist's model? Well, I never,' said Paul, the jockey, as he led his horse along the street.

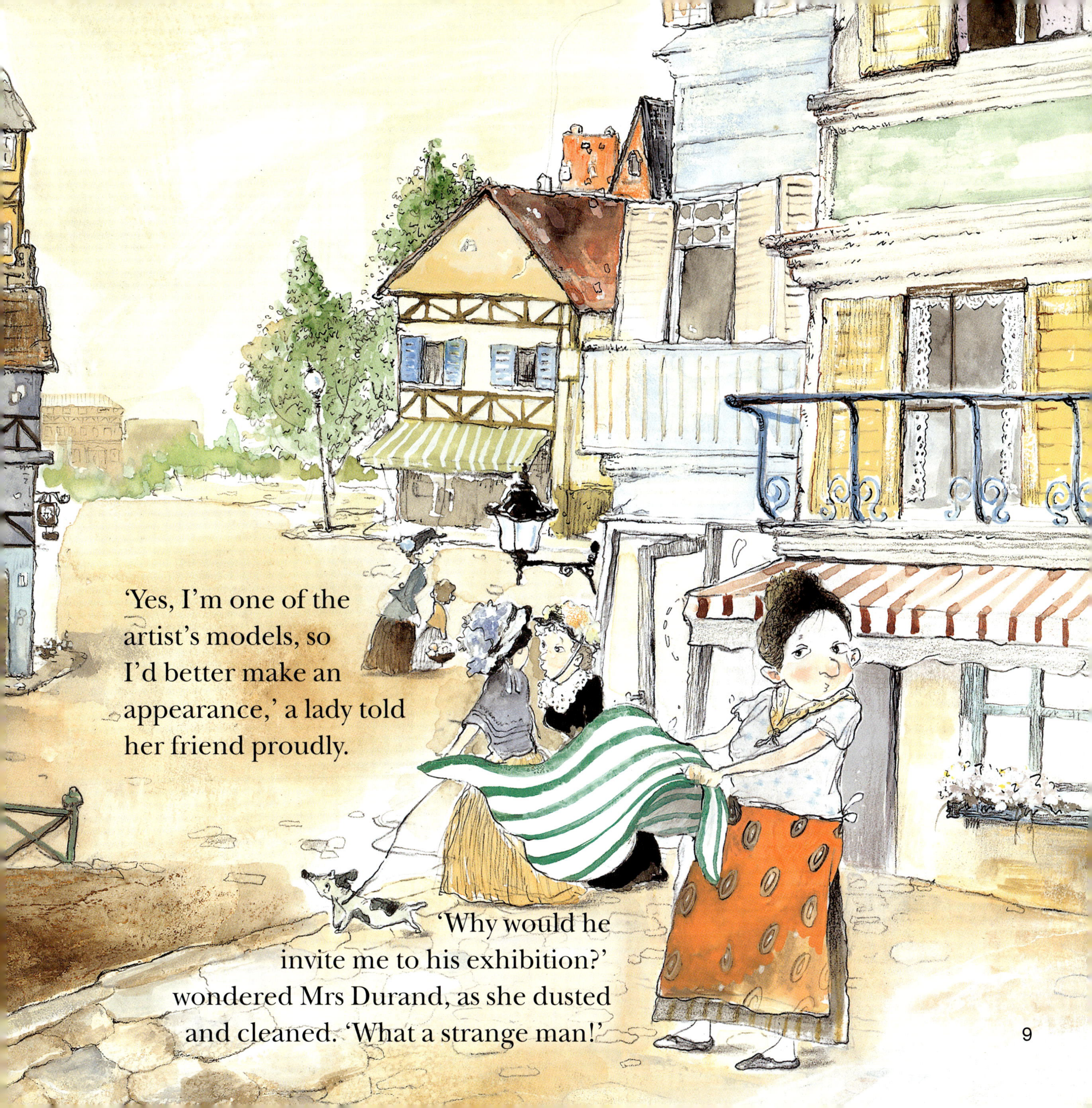

'Yes, I'm one of the artist's models, so I'd better make an appearance,' a lady told her friend proudly.

'Why would he invite me to his exhibition?' wondered Mrs Durand, as she dusted and cleaned. 'What a strange man!'

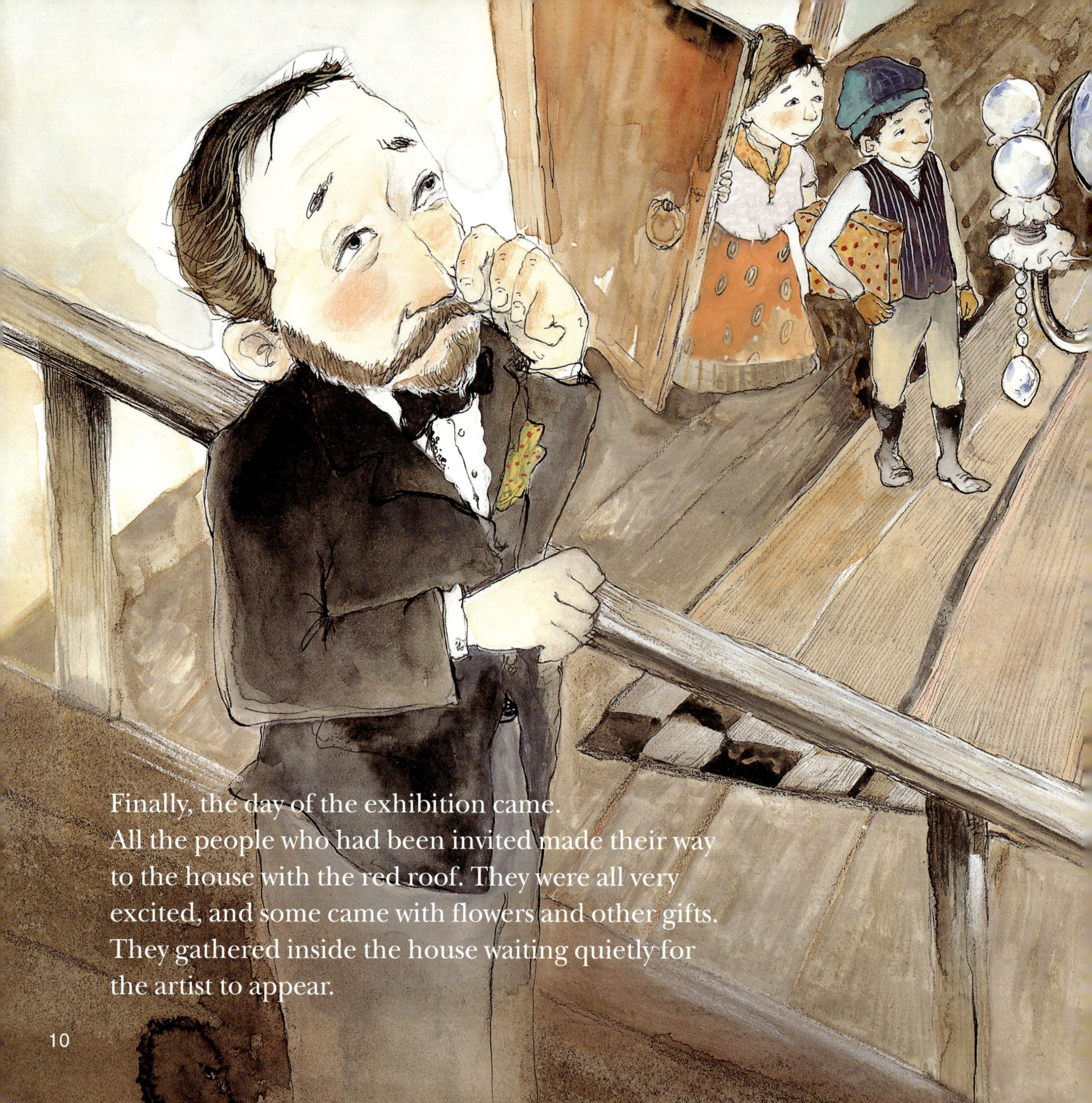

Finally, the day of the exhibition came. All the people who had been invited made their way to the house with the red roof. They were all very excited, and some came with flowers and other gifts. They gathered inside the house waiting quietly for the artist to appear.

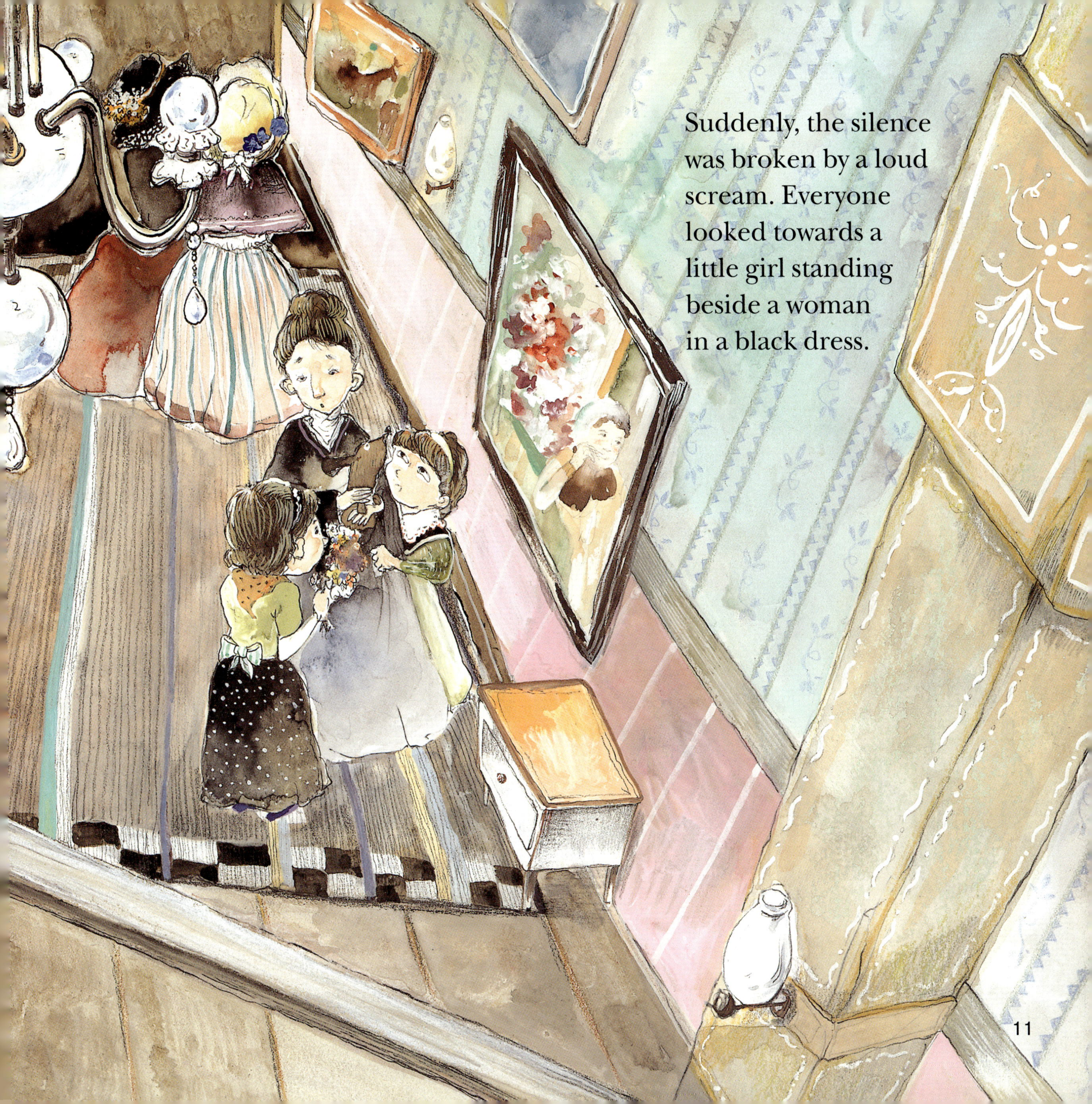

Suddenly, the silence was broken by a loud scream. Everyone looked towards a little girl standing beside a woman in a black dress.

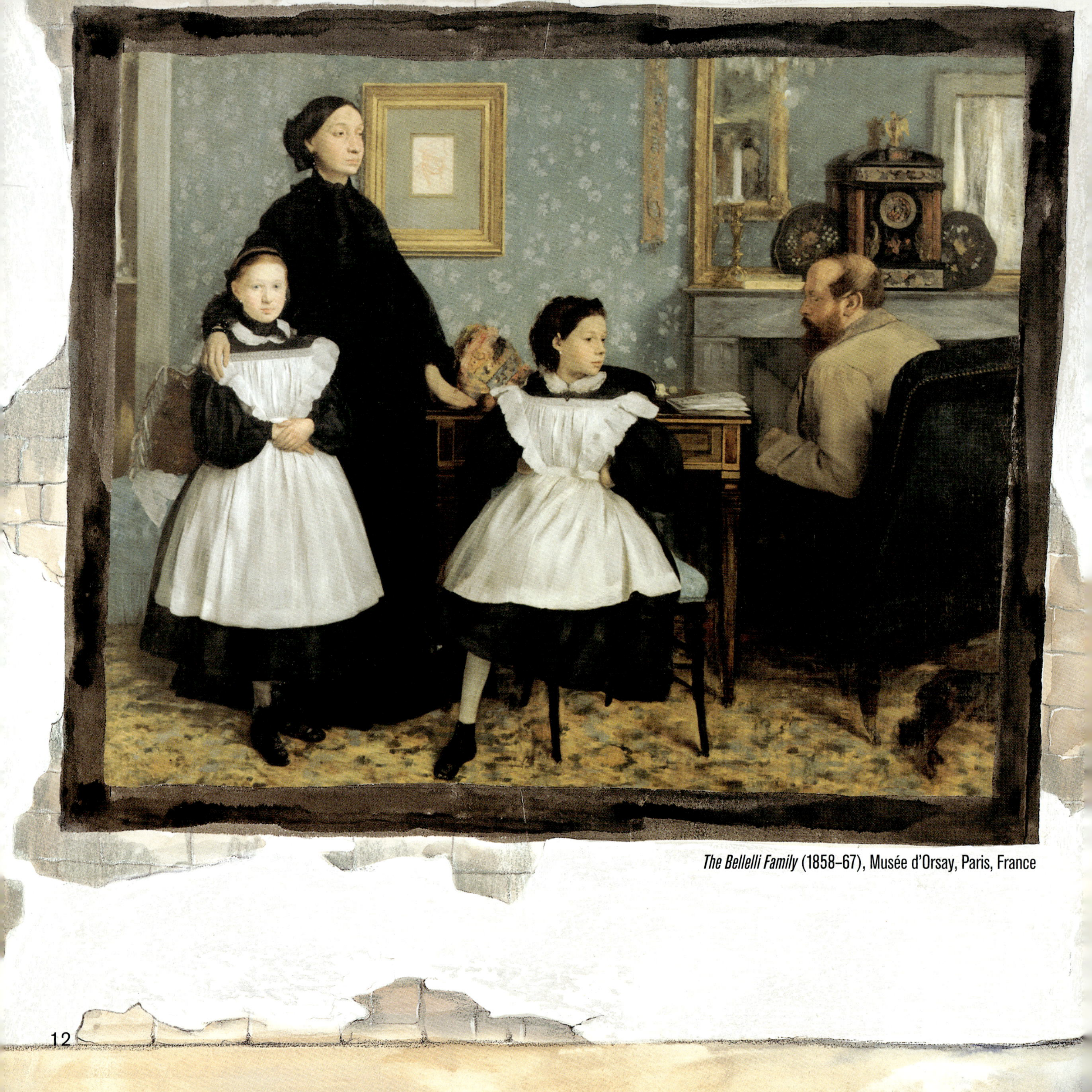

*The Bellelli Family* (1858–67), Musée d'Orsay, Paris, France

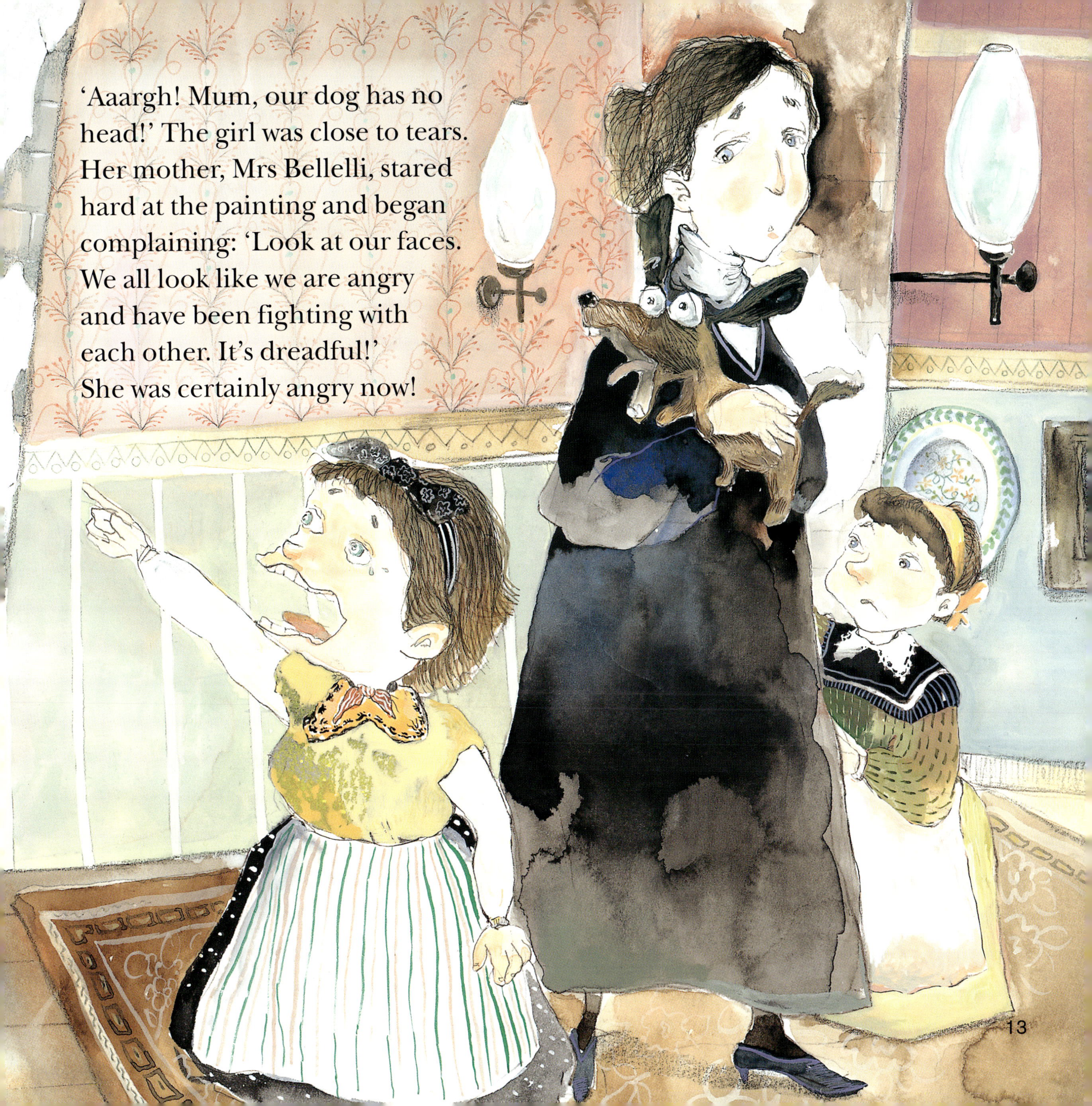

‘Aaargh! Mum, our dog has no head!’ The girl was close to tears. Her mother, Mrs Bellelli, stared hard at the painting and began complaining: ‘Look at our faces. We all look like we are angry and have been fighting with each other. It’s dreadful!’ She was certainly angry now!

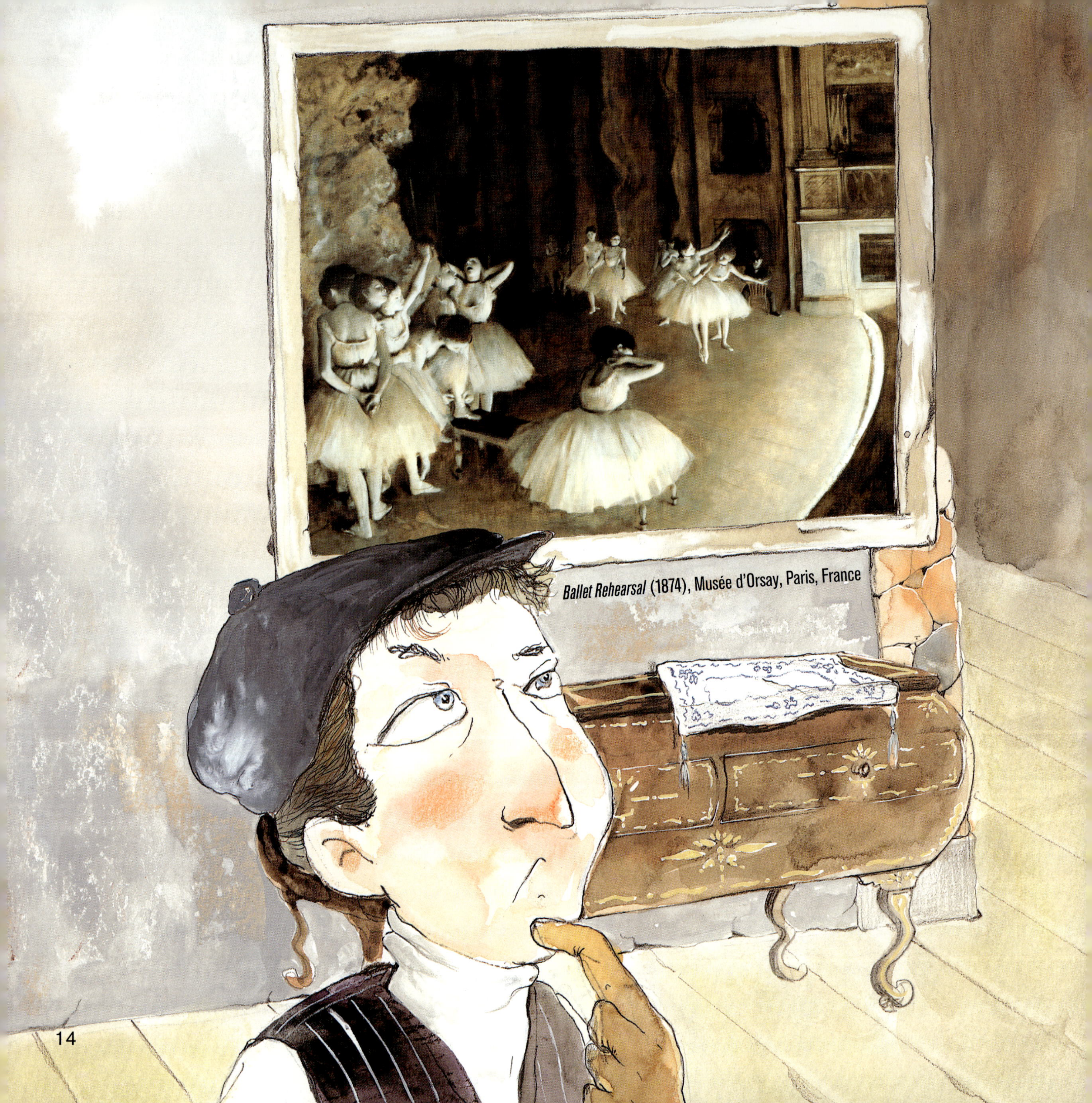

*Ballet Rehearsal* (1874), Musée d'Orsay, Paris, France

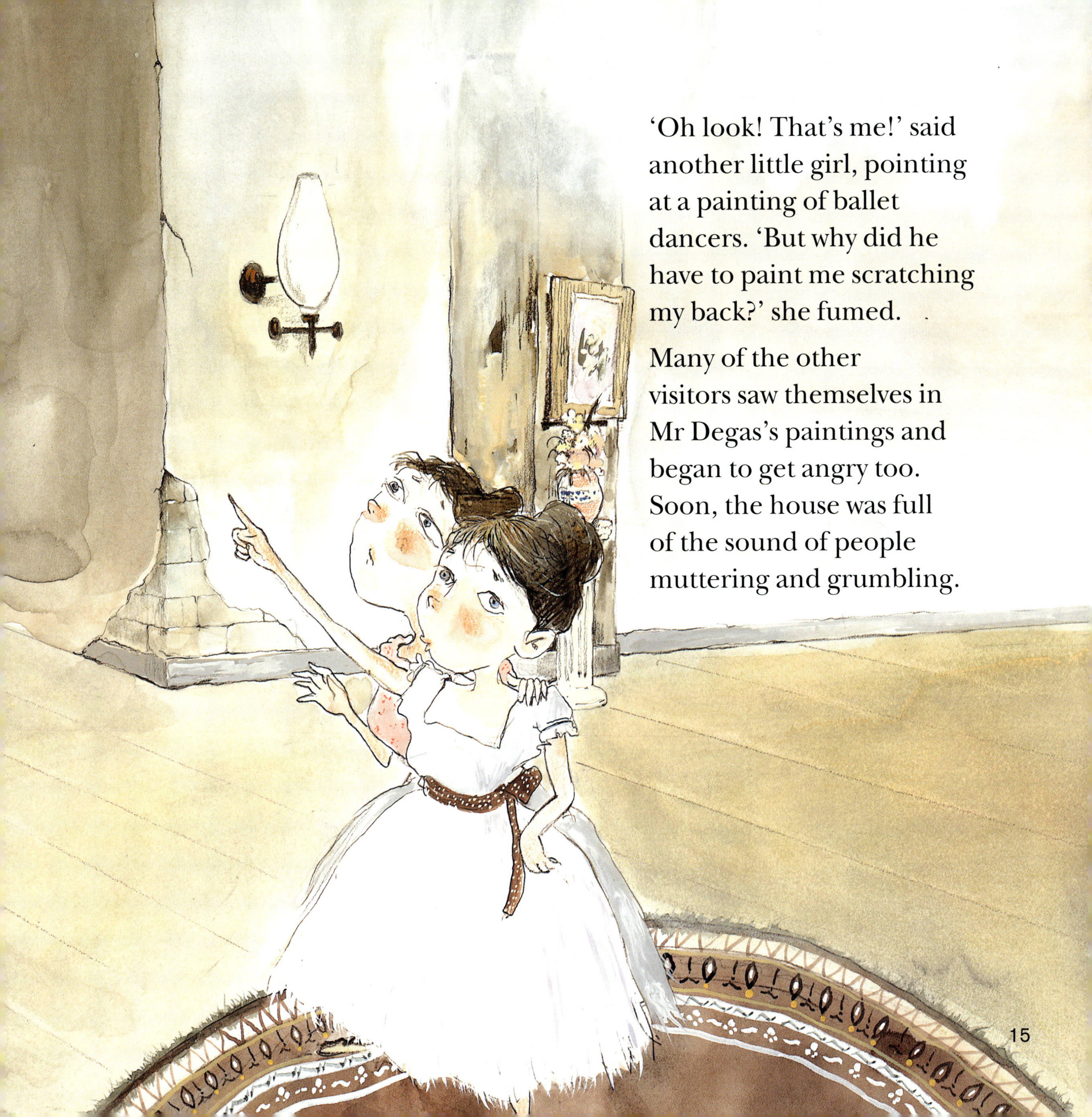

'Oh look! That's me!' said another little girl, pointing at a painting of ballet dancers. 'But why did he have to paint me scratching my back?' she fumed.

Many of the other visitors saw themselves in Mr Degas's paintings and began to get angry too. Soon, the house was full of the sound of people muttering and grumbling.

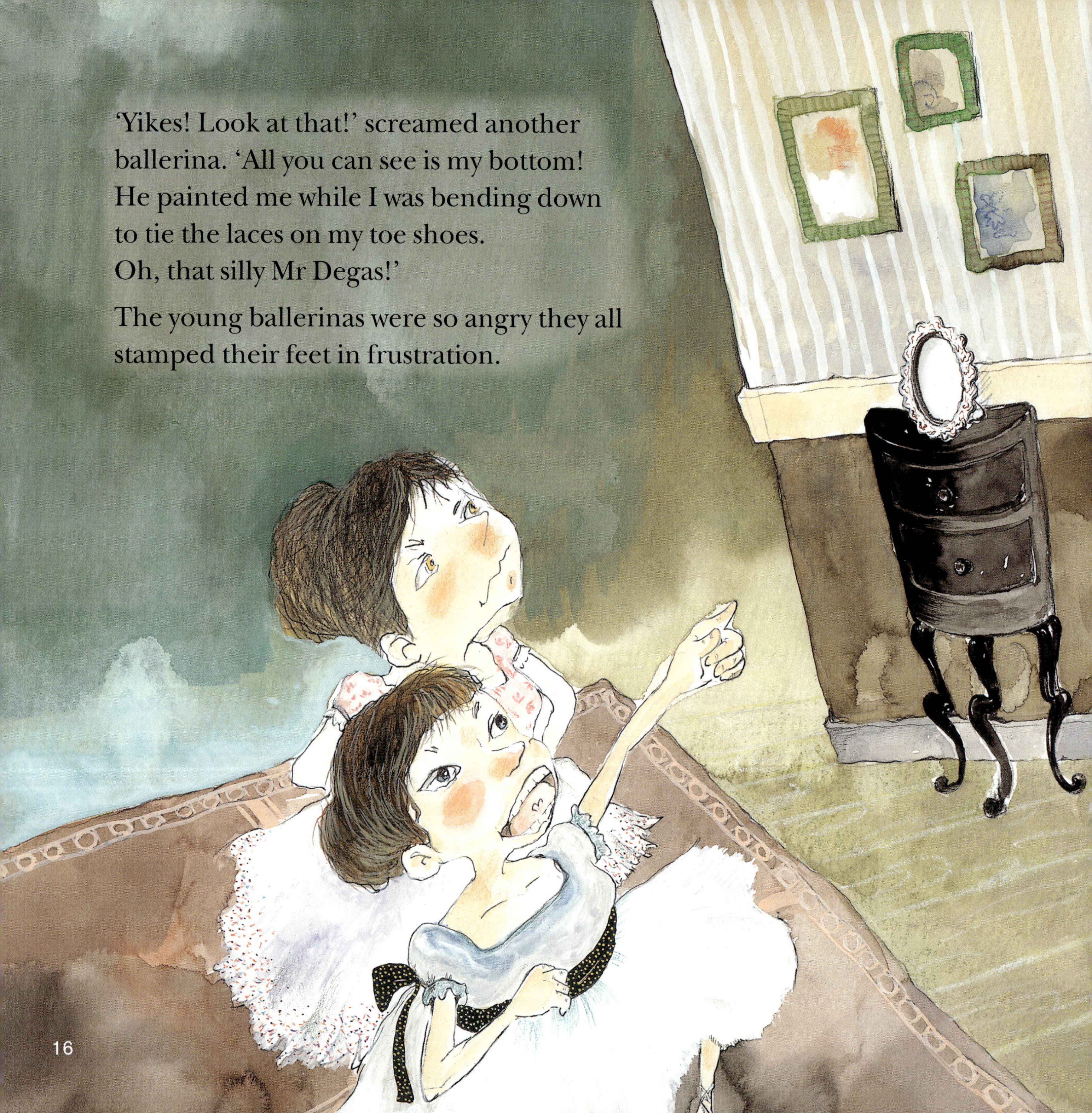

'Yikes! Look at that!' screamed another ballerina. 'All you can see is my bottom! He painted me while I was bending down to tie the laces on my toe shoes. Oh, that silly Mr Degas!'

The young ballerinas were so angry they all stamped their feet in frustration.

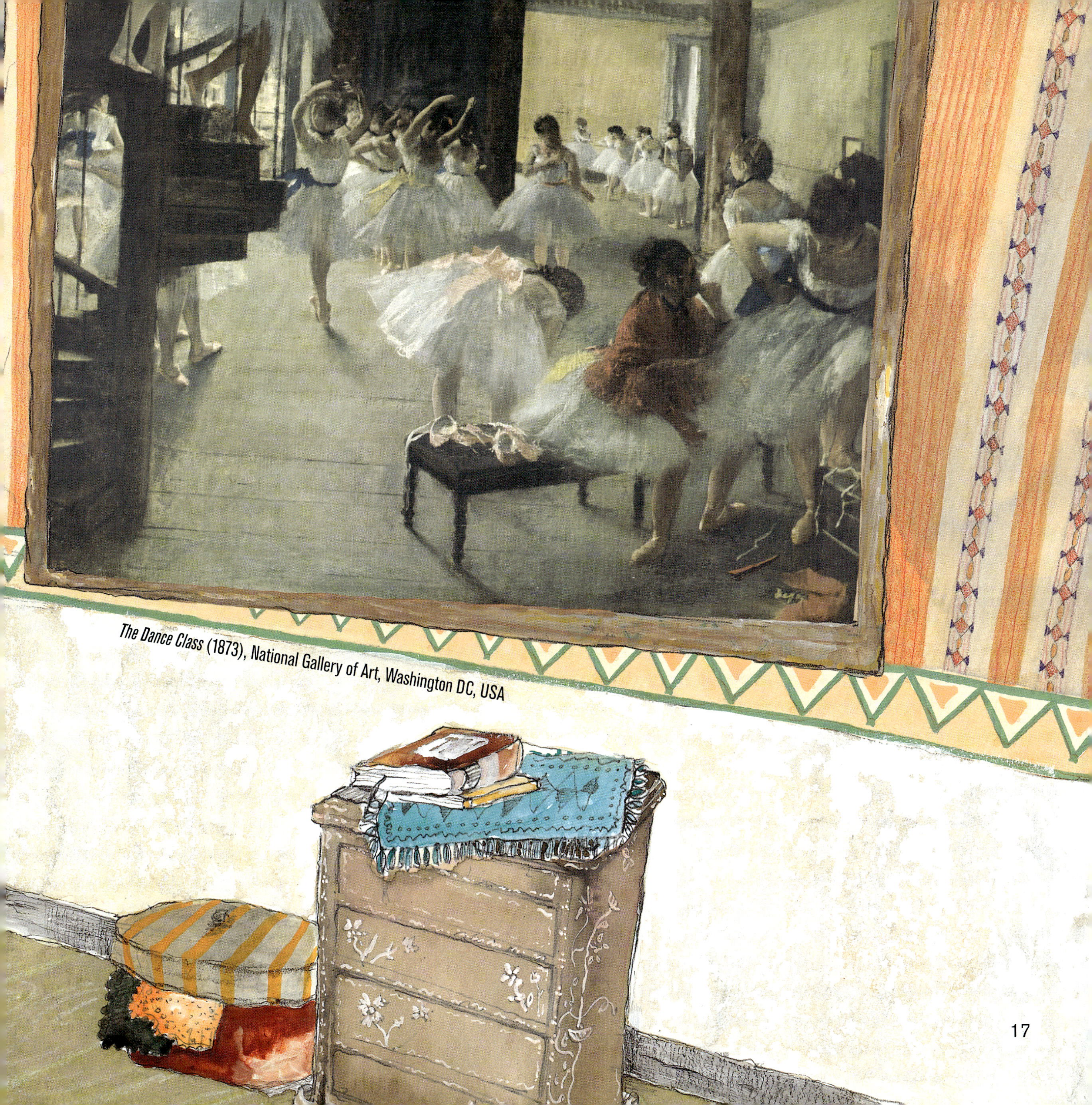

*The Dance Class* (1873), National Gallery of Art, Washington DC, USA

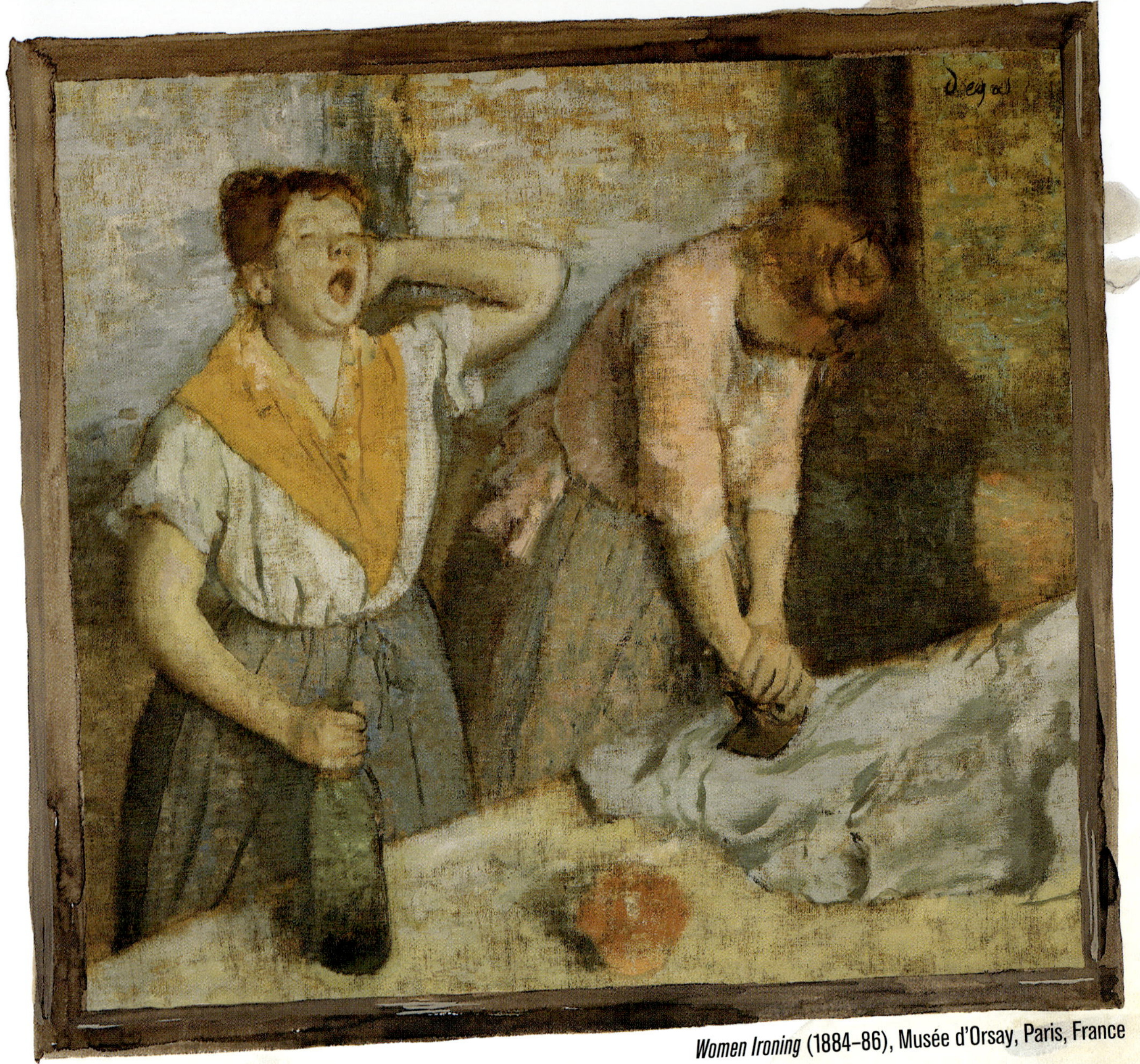

*Women Ironing* (1884–86), Musée d'Orsay, Paris, France

'Oh my goodness! When on earth did he paint this?' Mrs Durand stared at the painting with wide eyes. 'Now I see. He must have spied on us when we were doing the ironing. But why did he have to show me yawning? How embarrassing!'

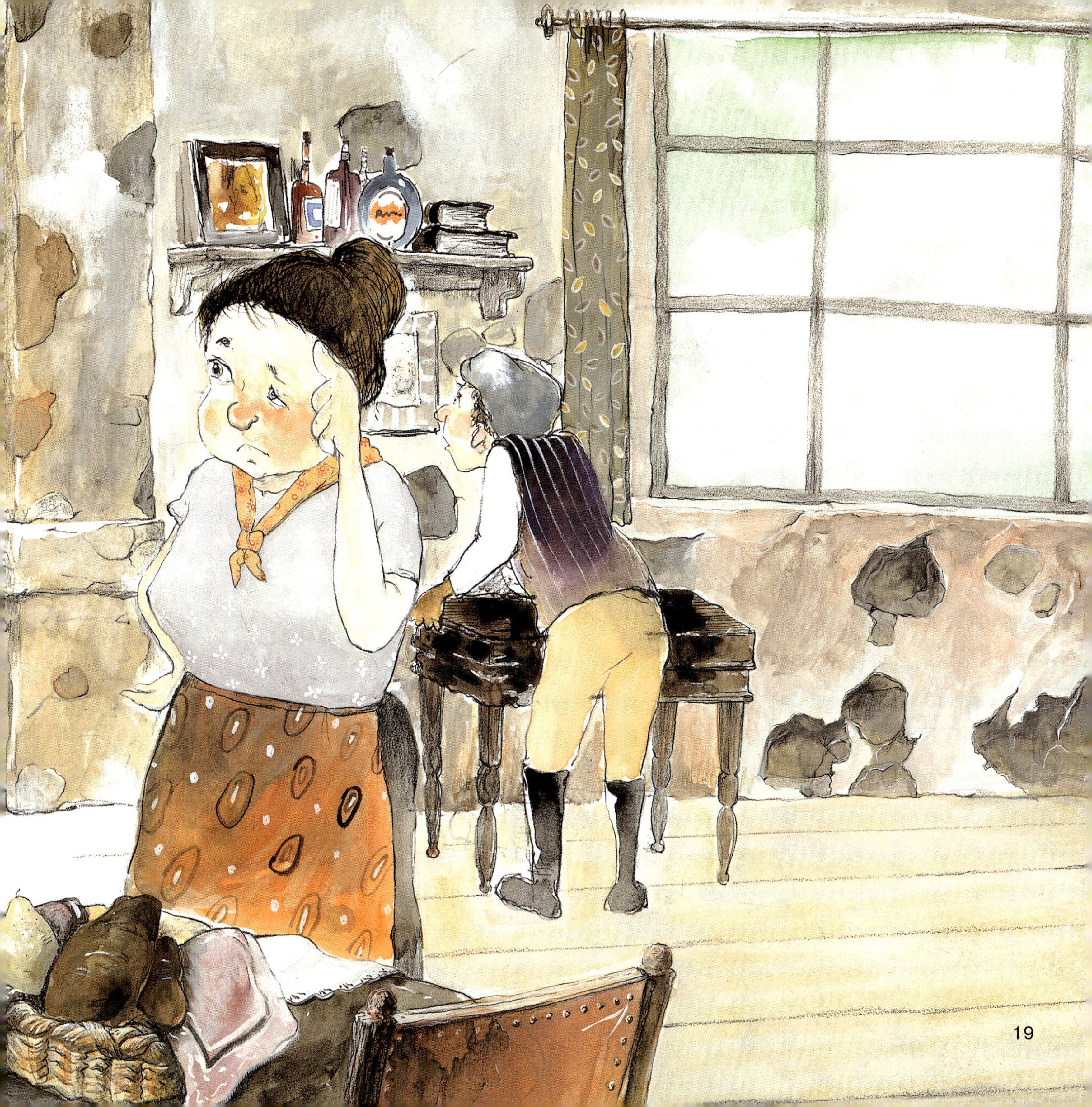

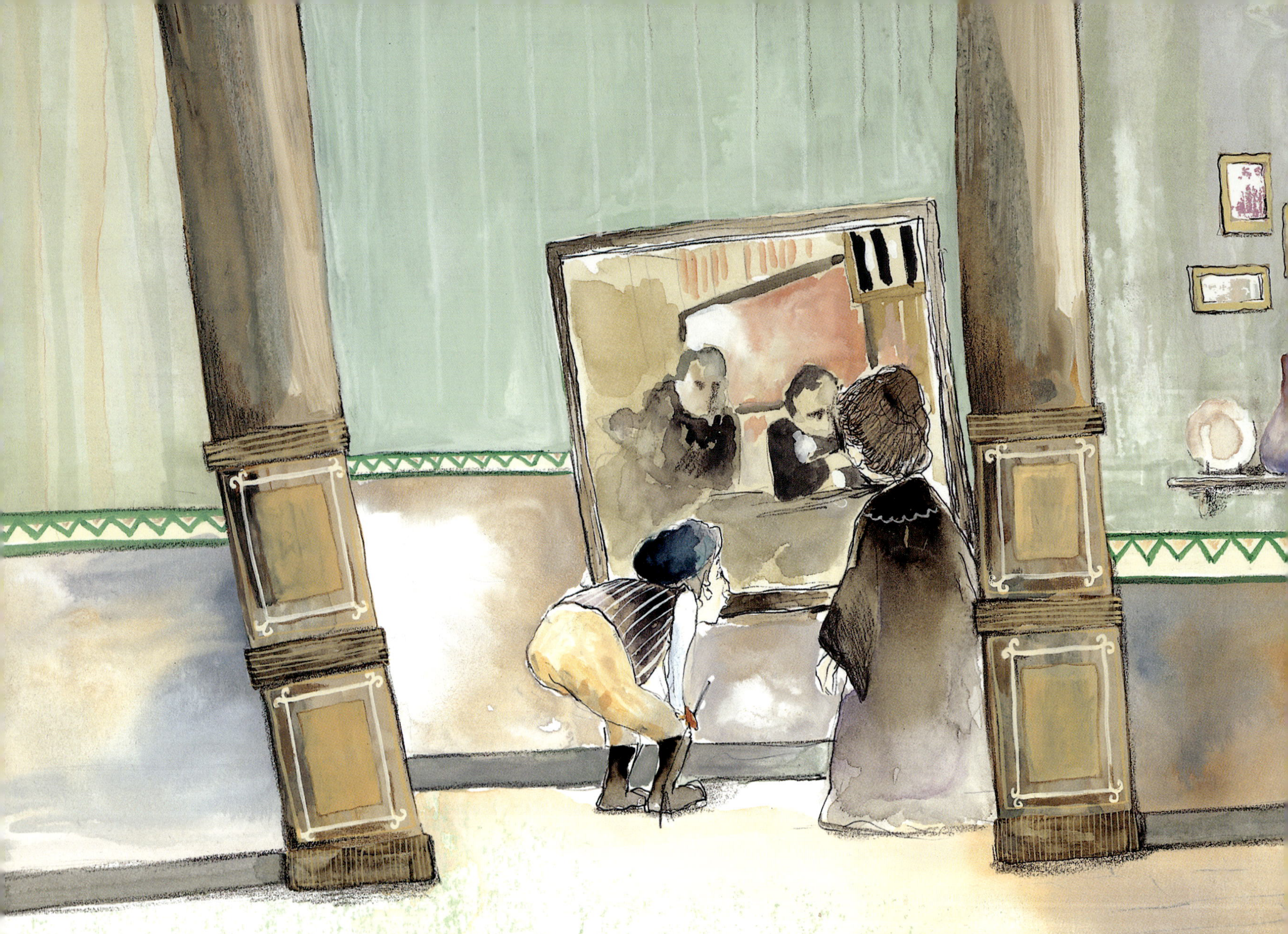

'Well, at least he managed to make *you* look beautiful, Hortense,' said Mrs Luno.

'Huh!' said Hortense. 'Beautiful maybe, but I had to stand still for hours while he painted me, and I got cramps in my feet. At least the others could just get on with what they were doing.'

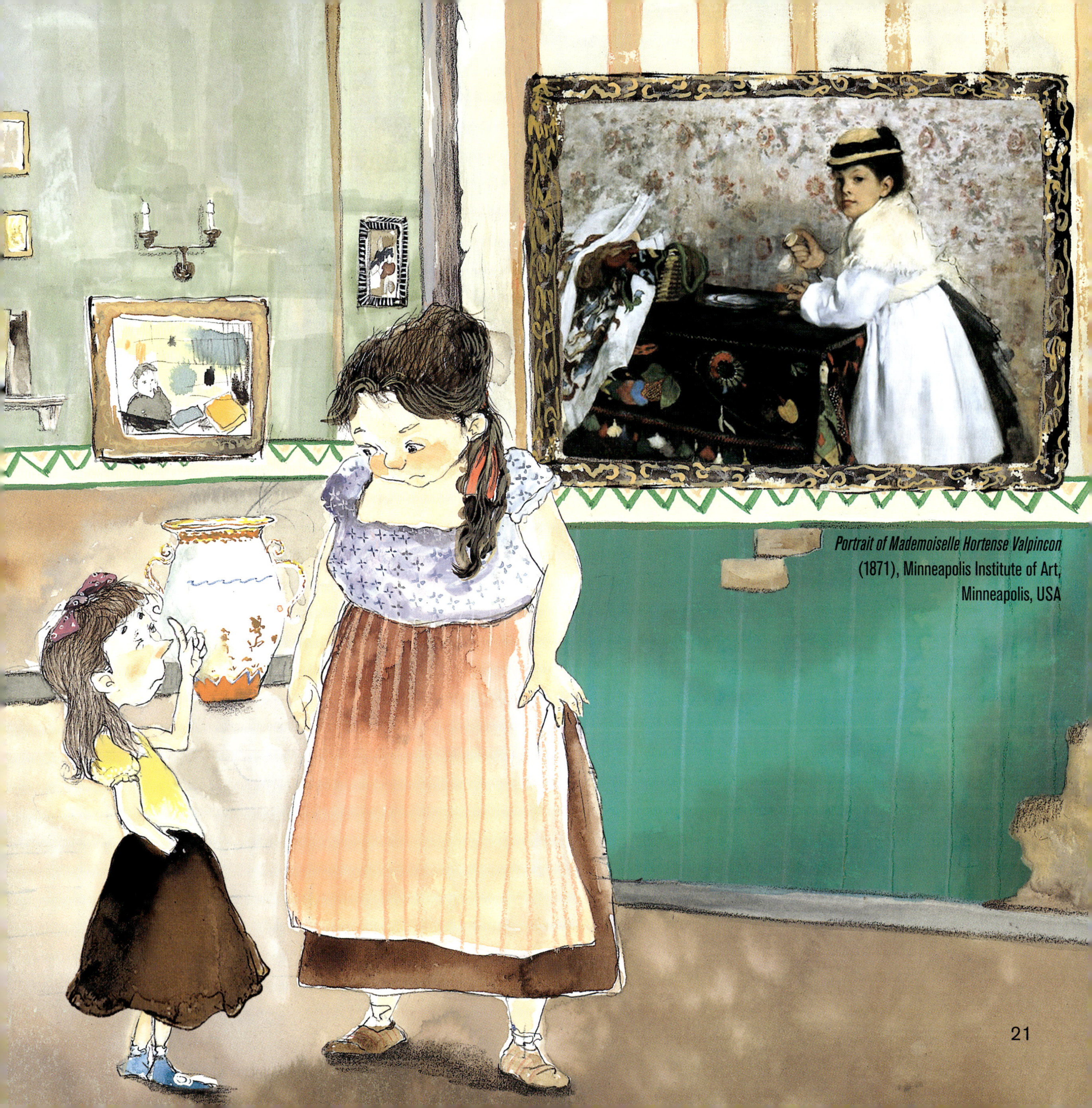

*Portrait of Mademoiselle Hortense Valpinçon*
(1871), Minneapolis Institute of Art,
Minneapolis, USA

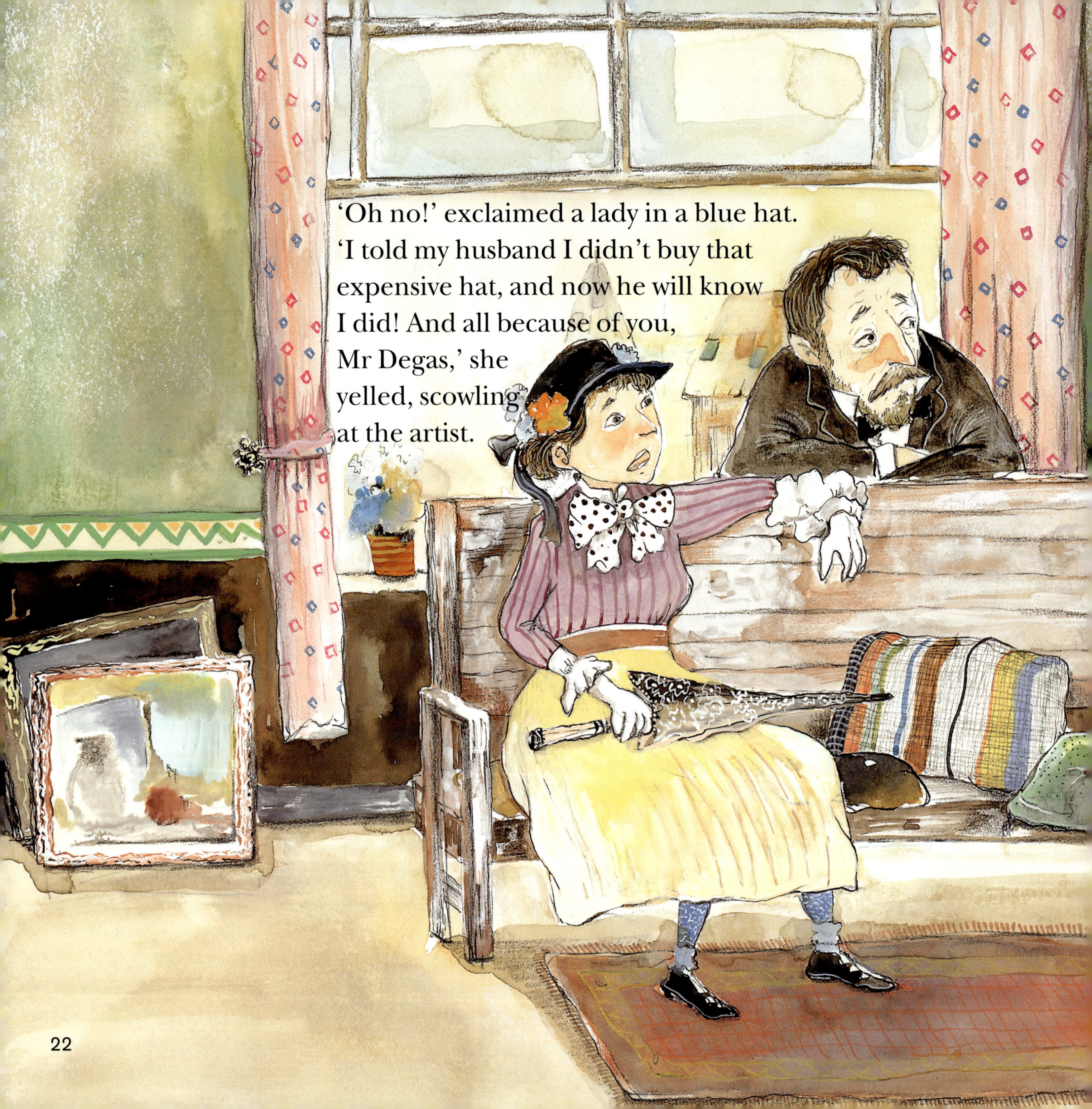

'Oh no!' exclaimed a lady in a blue hat. 'I told my husband I didn't buy that expensive hat, and now he will know I did! And all because of you, Mr Degas,' she yelled, scowling at the artist.

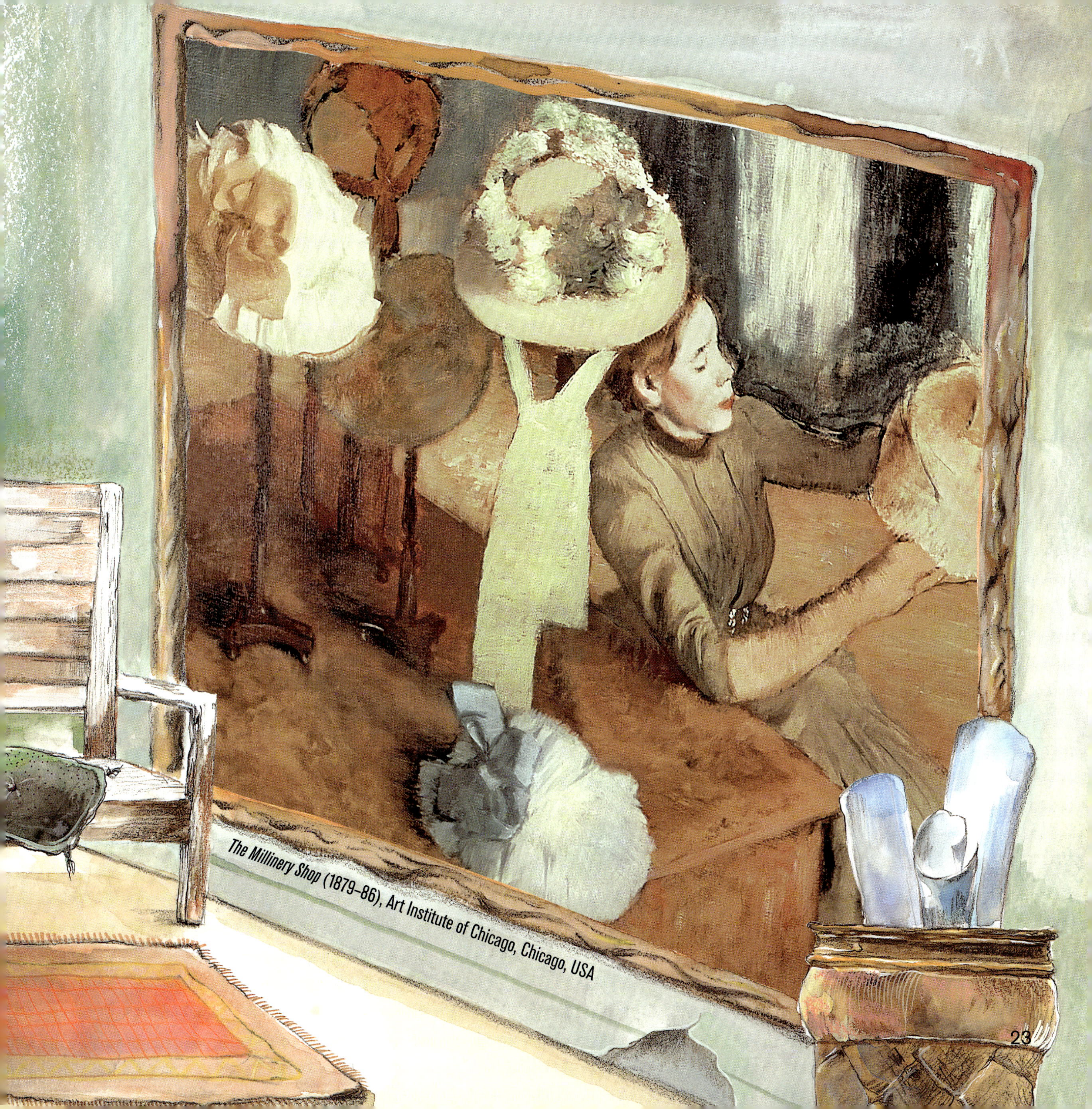

*The Millinery Shop* (1879–86), Art Institute of Chicago, Chicago, USA

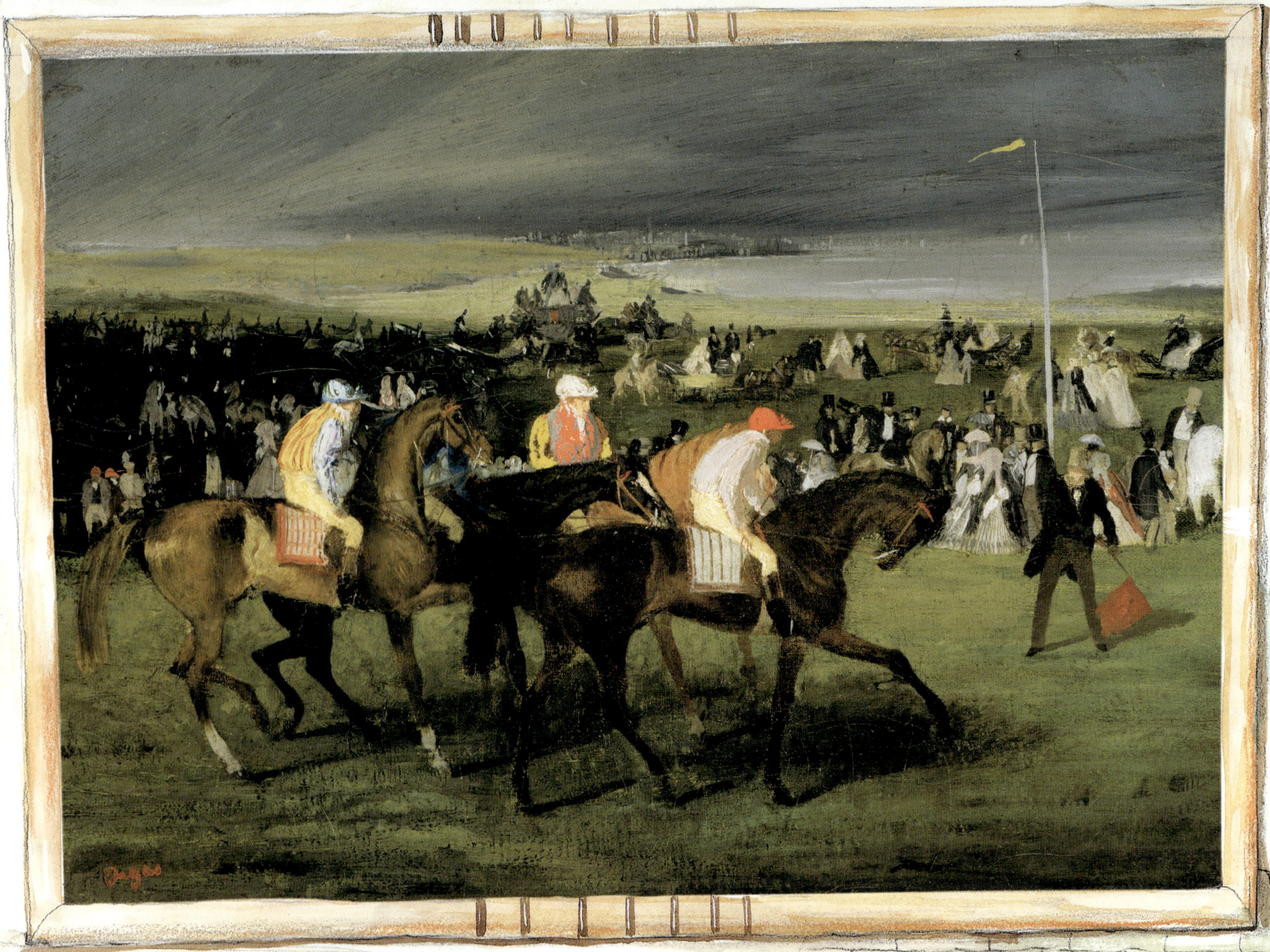

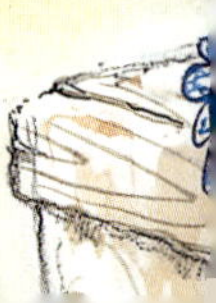

*At the Races: The Start* (1860–62), Fogg Museum, Cambridge, USA

'I'm not sure I like being painted without knowing about it,' said Paul, the jockey. 'But I have to admit that the way he has painted the horses running is amazing. It's so life-like!'

When Mr Degas heard that, he smiled and felt quietly proud.

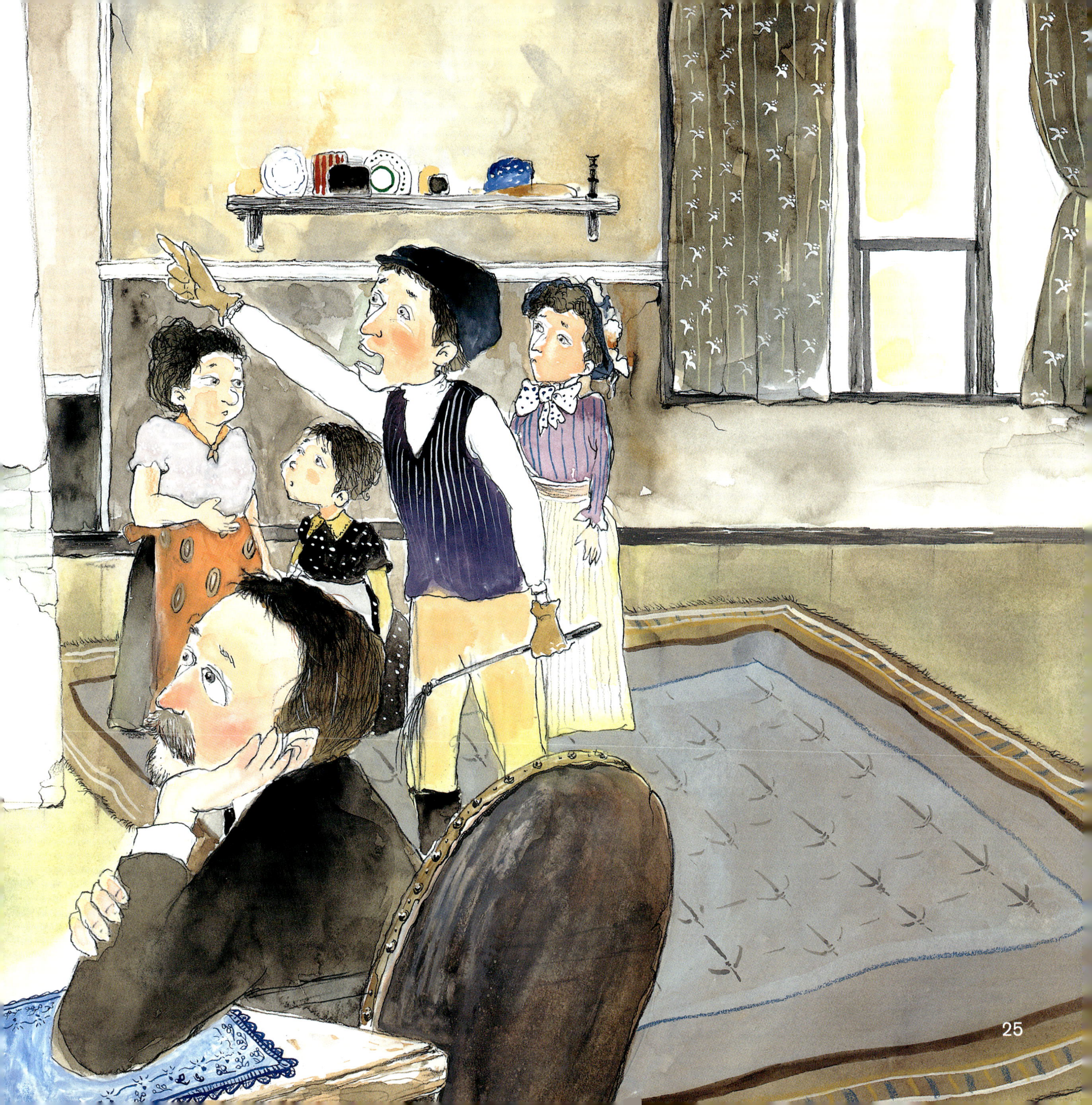

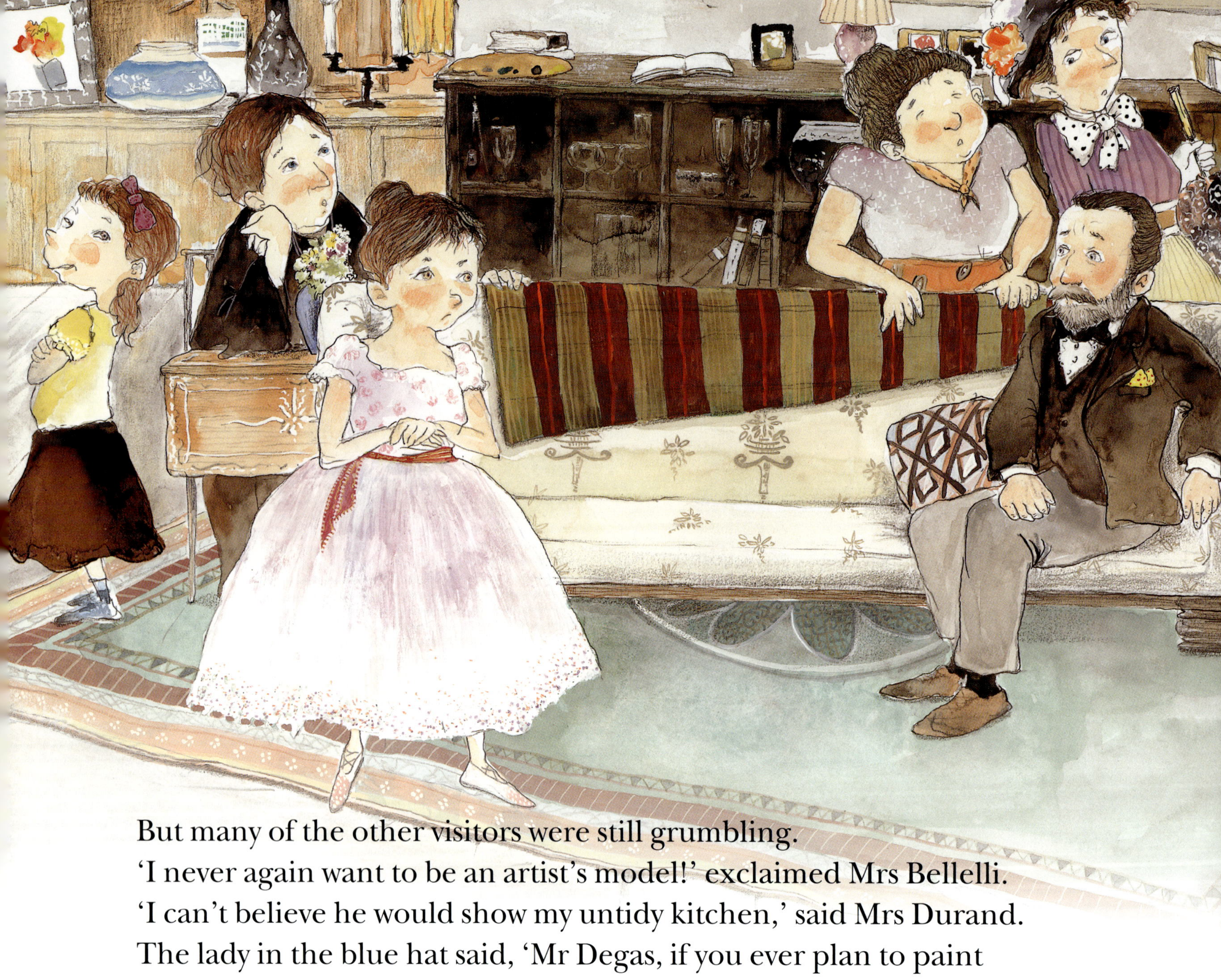

But many of the other visitors were still grumbling.
'I never again want to be an artist's model!' exclaimed Mrs Bellelli.
'I can't believe he would show my untidy kitchen,' said Mrs Durand.
The lady in the blue hat said, 'Mr Degas, if you ever plan to paint us again, please ask for our permission first!'
And one of the ballerinas asked, 'Next time, Mr Degas, can you please make me as beautiful as Hortense?'

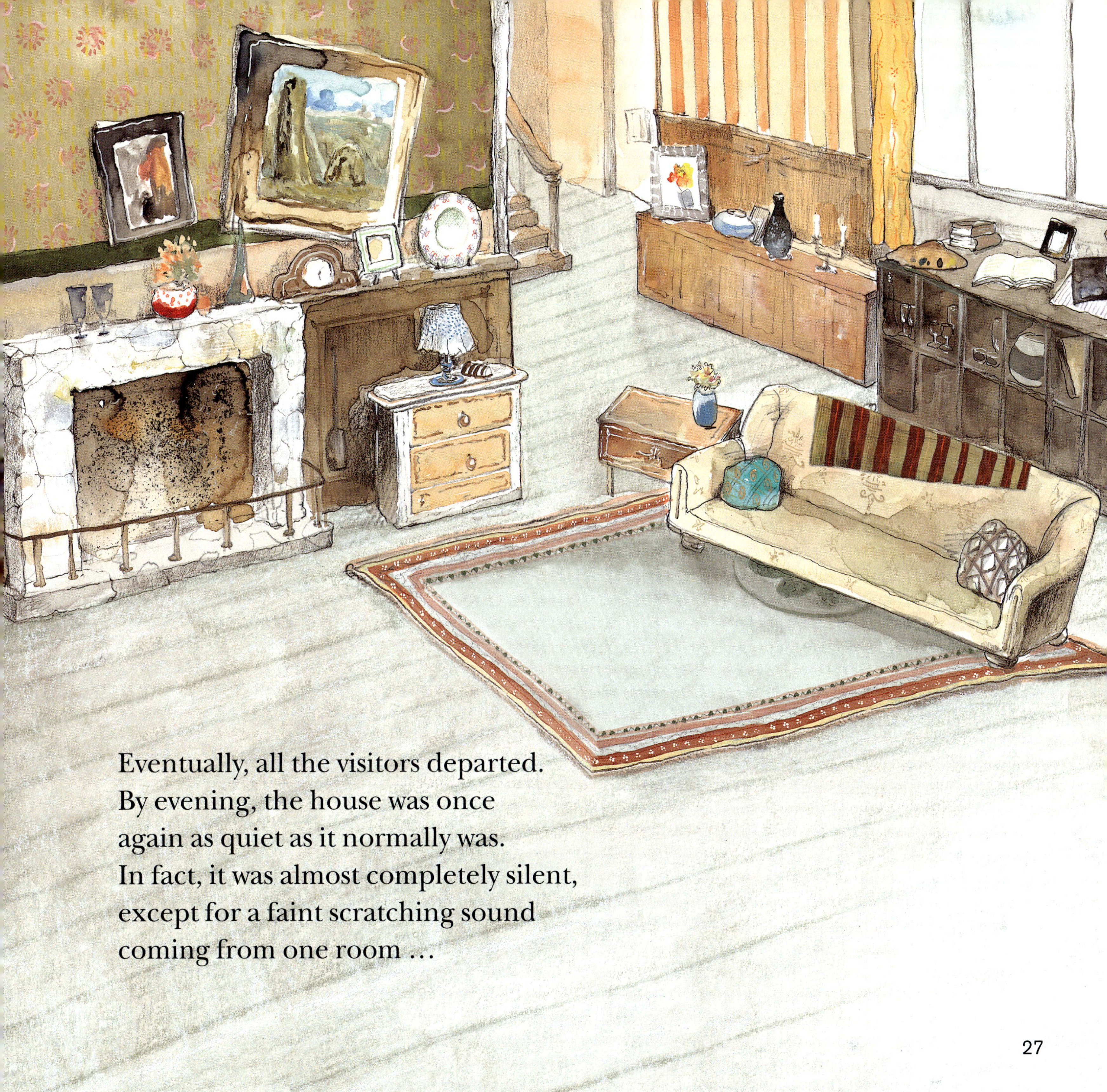

Eventually, all the visitors departed. By evening, the house was once again as quiet as it normally was. In fact, it was almost completely silent, except for a faint scratching sound coming from one room …

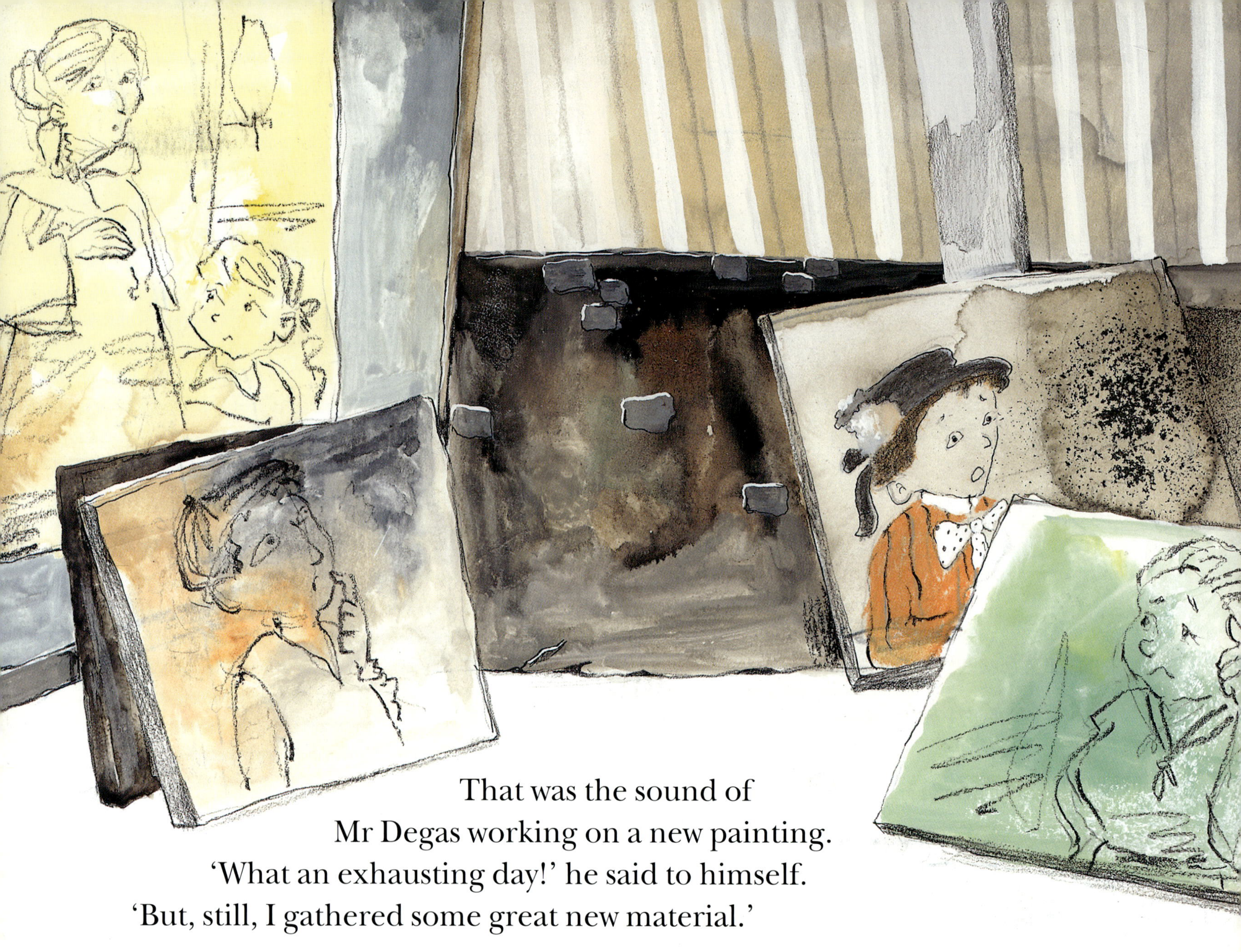

That was the sound of
Mr Degas working on a new painting.
'What an exhausting day!' he said to himself.
'But, still, I gathered some great new material.'

On the canvases around Mr Degas were sketches of Mrs Durand scratching her head, Paul the jockey looking puzzled, the ballerinas throwing a tantrum — and many more.

'Wait till they see my next exhibition!' he said, chuckling to himself.

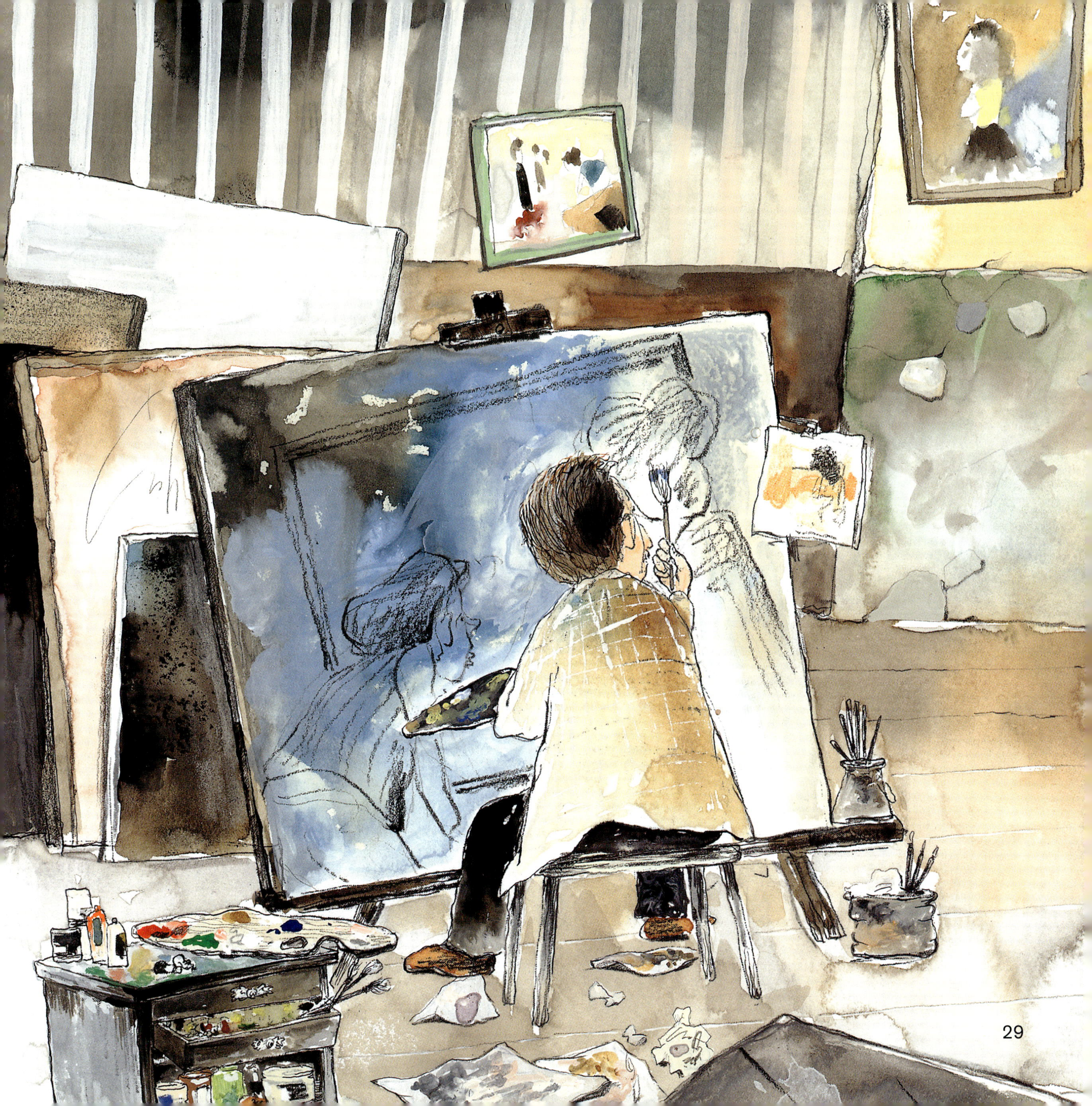

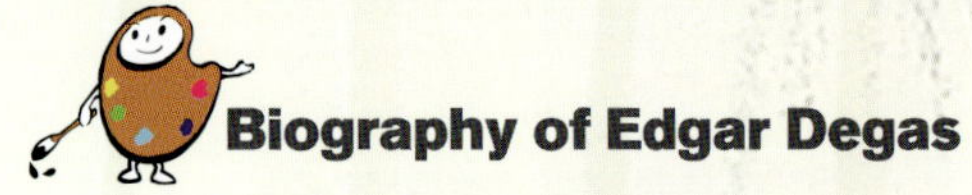



# Moments in time

Edgar Degas was born in Paris, France, in 1834. His father was a banker and his family was wealthy. Edgar grew into a shy and sensitive young man. He had few interests and didn't know what he wanted to do in life. Taking his parents' advice, he began to study law, but he did not enjoy it and dropped out of his course. Soon after, however, he discovered what he really wanted to do: become an artist.

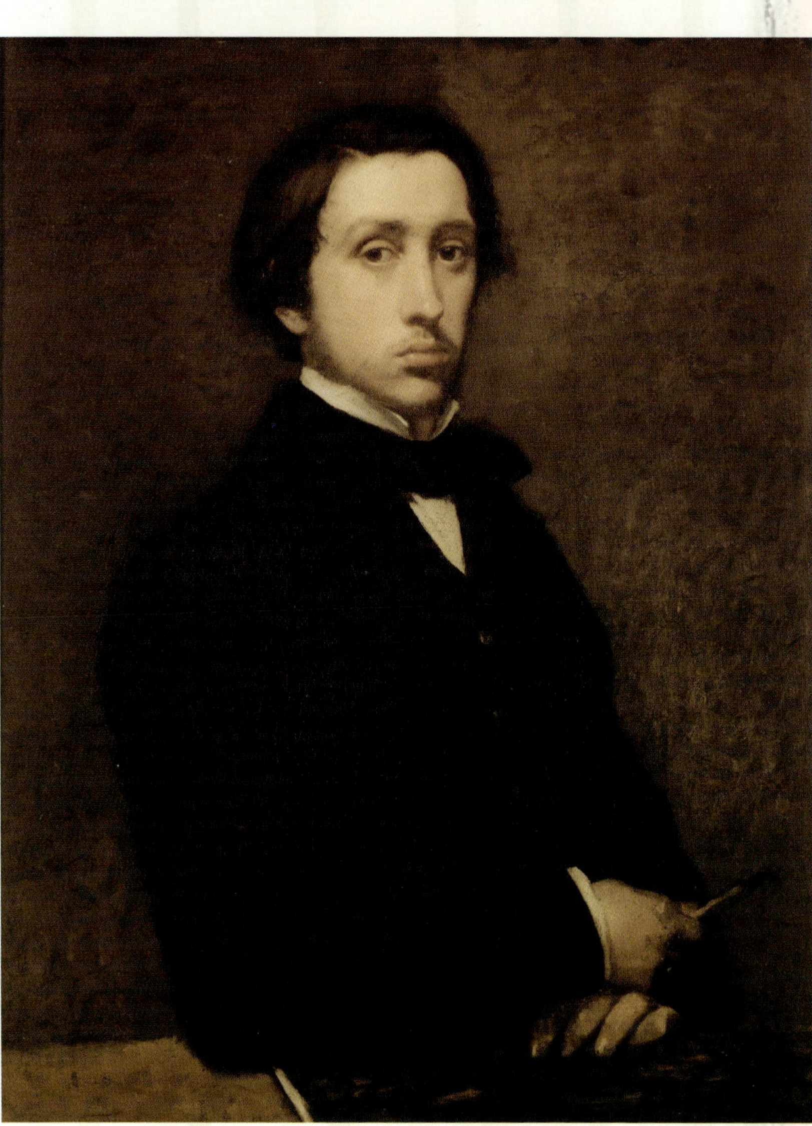

## Loving support

When Degas decided he wanted to be a painter, his father was not annoyed. Instead he was happy that his son had found something that he loved doing and was keen to do for the rest of his life. So he gave Edgar his full support.

Using money from his father, Degas travelled to Italy to look at paintings by the great masters of the Renaissance, that period in the late Middle Ages in Italy when painting flourished. He carefully studied works by artists such as Raphael and Michelangelo. Along with constant practice, his observation of their works helped him become a highly skilled painter.

On his return to Paris, Degas set up a studio. Increasingly, he liked to paint scenes from modern life, including horseracing. When, in 1870, Prussia attacked France, Degas helped defend the city. During 1872, he travelled to New Orleans in the United States to visit his brother René and other relatives.

*Self-portrait* (1855), Musée d'Orsay, Paris, France

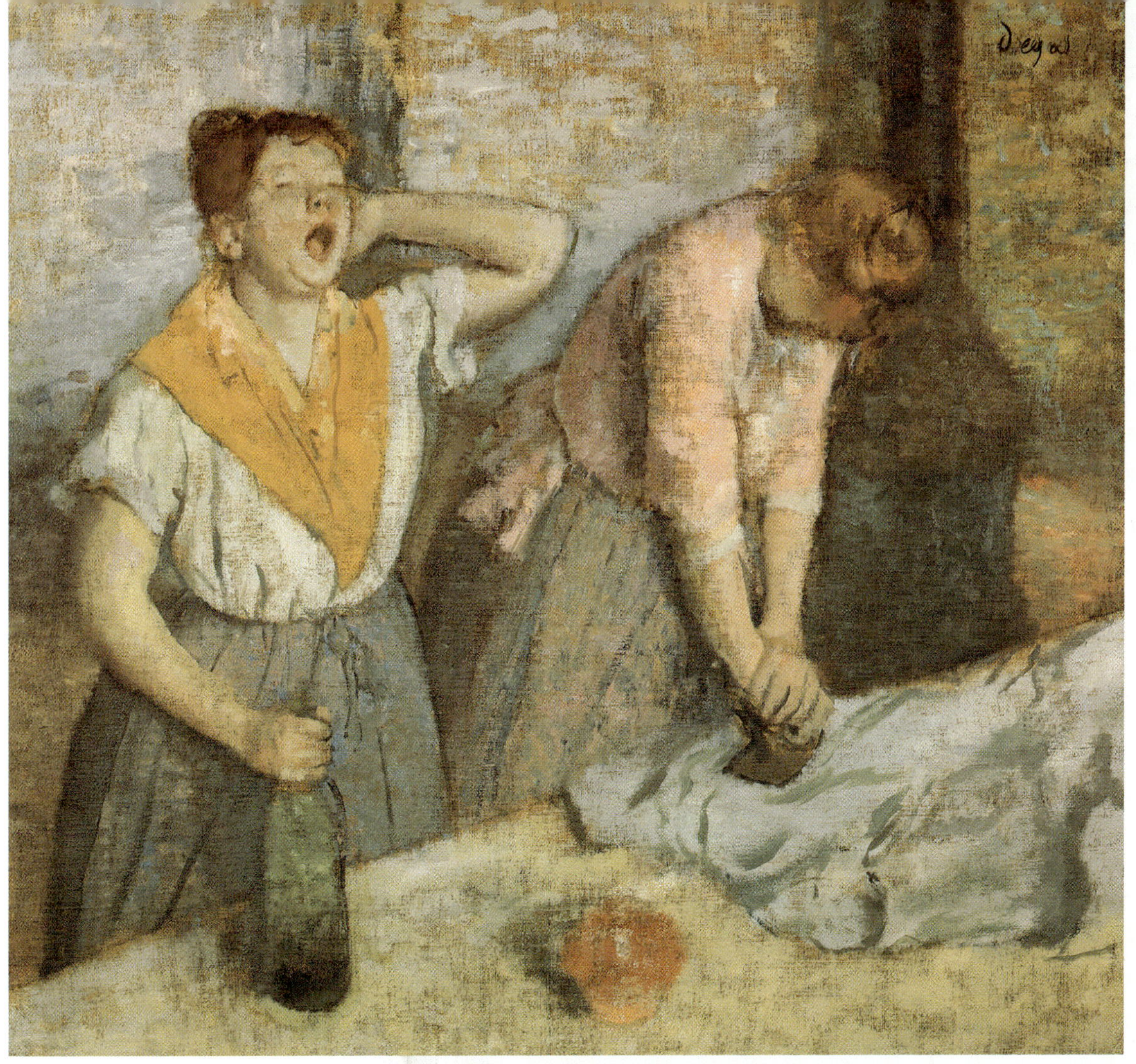

*Women Ironing* (1884–86), Musée d'Orsay, Paris, France

### Captured in an instant

Degas spent a lot of his time just quietly observing his subjects. After a while he would get to know them and identify their most distinctive features or habits. He could draw so well and so fast that when he saw his subject in a pose he wanted to paint, he could sketch it very quickly and capture that moment in time. It was almost like being able to take a photograph.

For instance, he painted a showgirl with a nervous look on her face just before she went on stage at a theatre. If he hadn't observed her so carefully, he would never have caught that expression.

And he painted the women ironing (above) when they least expected him to. One has her head down and is working hard, but the other is yawning and stretching. If he hadn't spent a lot of time with them, just observing, he would never have managed to show them in that way.

**1834**
Born on July 19 in Paris, France

**1855**
Enrols at art school

**1856**
Travels to Italy

**1860**
Begins painting racehorses

**1865**
Shows his works in a major Paris exhibition at the Salon

**1870**
France and Prussia go to war; Degas enlists in the national guard

**1874**
Exhibits his paintings in the Impressionist exhibitions

**1881**
Completes *The Little Fourteen-Year-Old Dancer*

**1911**
Has to stop working due to failing eyesight

**1917**
Dies on September 27

# Favourite subjects

Two of Degas's favourite subjects were ballet dancers and racehorses. He spent a lot of time at the theatre and at the racecourse, watching everything that was going on. His paintings of these places are very realistic, and he became highly skilled at showing the movements of dancers and racing horses.

Degas became interested in horses when he was a student, and began making studies of their bodies and movements. In the 1860s, he started visiting racecourses and sketching the horses and their brightly clothed jockeys. Eventually he made more than 45 paintings of racehorses, as well as 17 sculptures and hundreds of drawings.

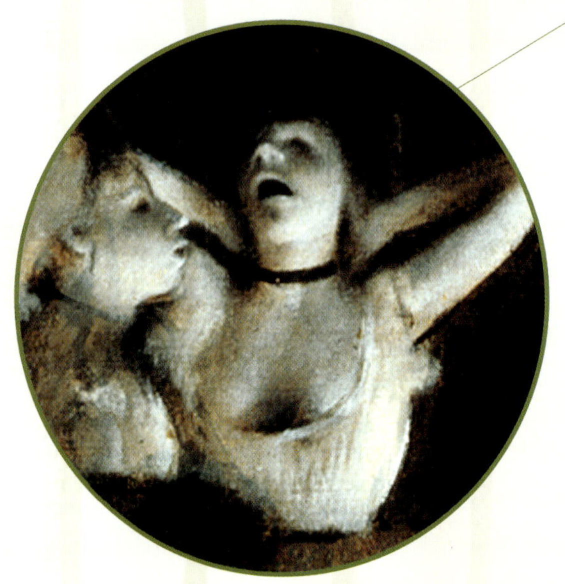

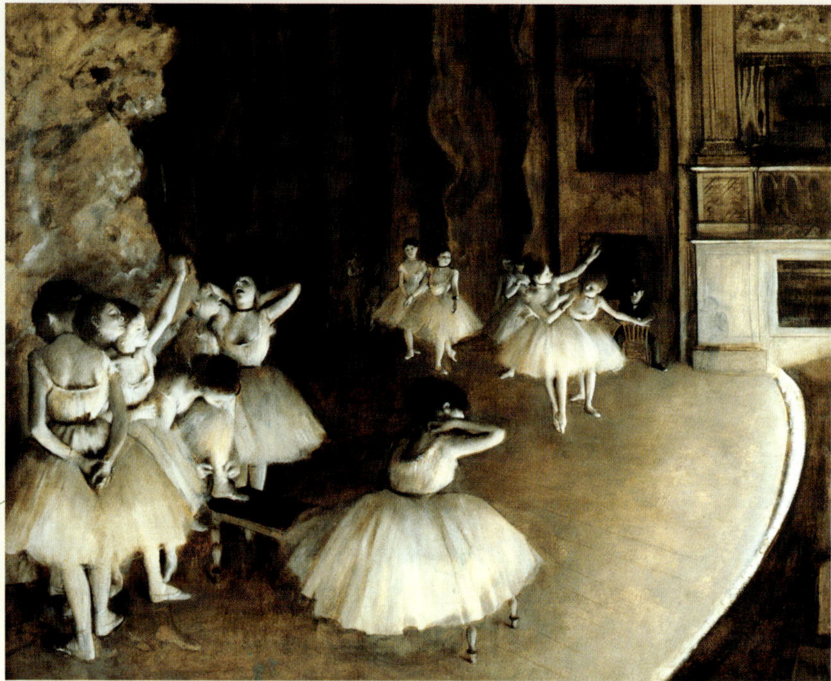

*Ballet Rehearsal* (1874), Musée d'Orsay, Paris, France

### Behind the scenes

In the 1870s, Degas regularly went to the Palais Garnier, home of the Paris Opera and the Paris Ballet, to watch the musicians and ballet dancers. He liked to observe them backstage, when they were rehearsing or getting ready to go on stage. He wanted to show the hard work involved in their performances.

Some of the dancers also came to Degas's studio to pose for him. Degas's paintings of musicians and ballet dancers became very popular and sold for high prices.

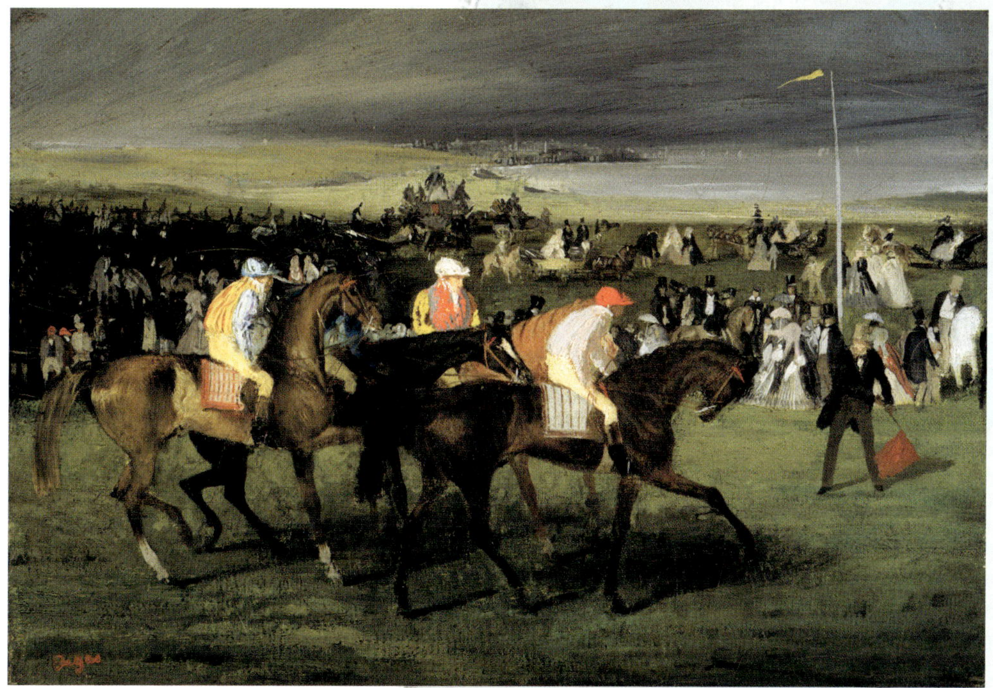

*At the Races: The Start* (1860–62), Fogg Museum, Cambridge, USA

## Turning to sculpture

Degas's works include sculptures as well as paintings. He turned to sculpture late in life after his eyesight weakened and he could no longer see colours clearly.

To some of his sculptures, like *The Little Fourteen-Year-Old Dancer*, Degas attached real clothes – in this case a skirt and even a hair ribbon. As in his paintings, the people in Degas's sculptures are shown in realistic, everyday poses. And, as with the paintings, their naturalness shocked some viewers.

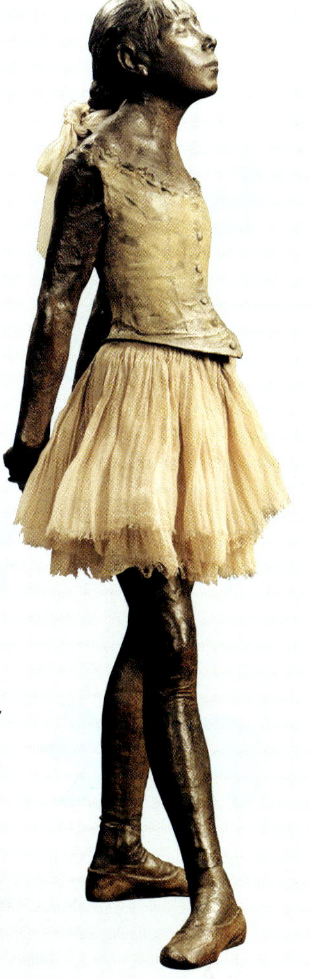

*The Little Fourteen-Year-Old Dancer* (1879–81), Musée d'Orsay, Paris, France

*'We don't always look our best in Mr Degas's art.*

*But I suppose it shows us as we really are!'*

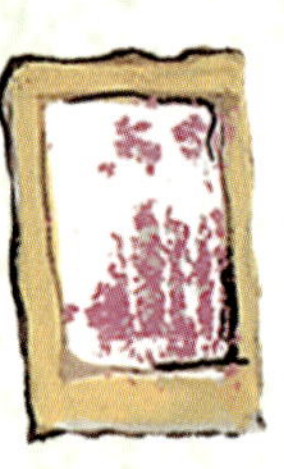

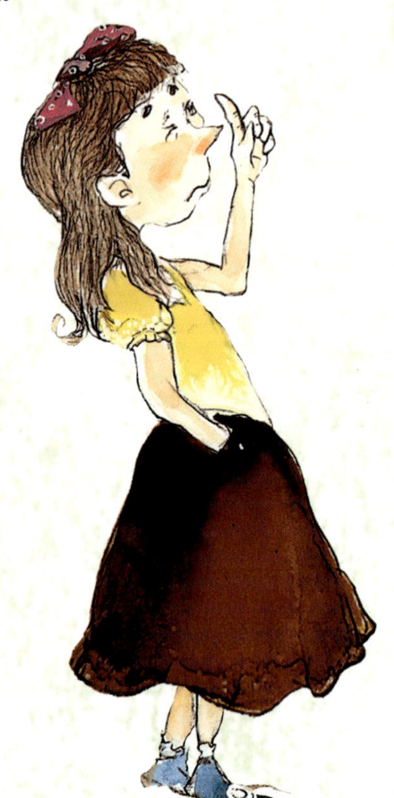